CRAIG CARSON   CHRIS NIHMEY

A Quarter Past Three

TREASURES OF TIME

Book II

Turtles Publishing
Ottawa, Canada

ISBN 0-9689125-1-6

Carson, Craig
Nihmey, Chris

A Quarter Past Three
Treasures of Time
Book II

September 2003
First Edition
Printed and Bound in Canada
By St. Joseph Print Group, Ottawa

We would like to thank God and our families for their guidance and support.

Table of Contents

INTRODUCTION

My name is Tommy, Tommy T. Timson, and I am lost in time. My adventure started one day after school when I was being chased by a couple of school bullies. I found a hiding place in an old hollowed oak tree, and when I crawled inside–POOF–I was sent back in time to the year 1215 AD.

So now I am lost in time and the series A Quarter Past Three is all about my attempts to get back home to the present. The first book is entitled Medieval Madness, and explains in detail what caused me to go back in time–I highly recommend it.

For those of you who haven't read the first book in the series, but plan on reading it eventually, I will tell you a little bit about my first adventure–but not enough to give it away. When I landed in the Middle Ages, I met a friendly wizard named Percival, who can't cook but does what he can to help me out. Percival told me that in order to get back home, I have to find magical doors and open them with magical keys that he provides. Each door leads to a different time period, until finally it will bring me back home. The only catch is that the magical doors appear for one minute, and if I'm not there, the doors will disappear leaving me lost in time forever! The doors appear at *a quarter past three* in the afternoon, which is the exact minute that I was sent back in time. This means that I have to hang out in my new surroundings for twenty-four hours before I can leave and that's when all the action happens. When I left the Middle Ages, I landed in the desert and the only things I could see were triangles in the distance and a caravan heading right for me! That's when this new book starts.

Sometimes I end up in places where the language is different from mine, so Percival has fixed things so that I can understand and communicate with all the people I encounter, which was really nice of him to do. He also told me of a girl my age who is also lost in time. I don't know much about her, but I hope to meet her some day so I can talk to someone who will actually believe all of this.

I should also mention that I have a sister named Tina, because I talk about her sometimes. One last thing, at the beginning of this book, I talk about smelling like sewage and that's because in the first book I had to go for a swim in some. Oh, and my favourite cookies are oatmeal.

Bye for now,

Tommy T. Timson

P.S. You will notice several bolded words in the story. There's a glossary with these words at the back of the book to help you understand the time period better.

1

Sandy Pants

It was 3:20 pm. The sun beat down and grew brighter with every passing second, its rays reflecting off the sand, blurring my vision. My jeans were too hot for the desert, so I dug around my bag for my shorts and remembered that I had forgotten them in the change room after gym class. I took off my jacket that was now full of sand, and as I shook it, I realized that I no longer smelled of rotten sewage and that my clothes were clean. I looked at myself and found that all the filth had disappeared. In its place was a lemony scent that was fresh and delicious! Cool! Time travelling cleans your clothes. I removed my watch and put it in my jeans pocket so that nobody would see it and then put my jacket in my bag.

The caravan was still headed my way and I could hear people shouting and yelling at each other as they pointed at me. They were getting closer and I was really scared. I just knew I had to get away from them. I pried one foot from the sand and slowly stepped backwards. "Whoa!" I stumbled and fell into a large crevasse that was behind me. I lay on my back motionless, stunned from the fall but unhurt, thanks to my backpack which softened the fall.

I crept up the side of the crevasse and peered over the crest. "YIKES!" I jerked my head down like a scared chicken. The caravan was almost on top of me, and they weren't riding camels, they were riding horses!

I stood up and dived to the other side of the crevasse. Covered with sweat, I slowly crawled up the side and finally pulled myself out. I was full of sand, but there wasn't any time to worry about that. I spit what I could from my mouth, brushed my ears and face with my hands, and started to run as fast as I could away from the caravan. I ran towards the triangular shaped structures I could see in the distance, but felt dizzy as the sun continued to roast me. My mouth was dry and I was thirsty, but to my surprise nobody was selling any lemonade.

So here I was, Tommy T. Timson, loved by his parents, adored by his teachers (for the most part), a good friend to many, struggling through a hot desert in who-knows-where, running for his life!

I continued to thrash through the sand, one foot at a time. If I reached the triangles I could hide, but I turned back to take a quick look and found that my pursuers were right behind me! The sand was so thick that each step slowed me down. It was like trudging through a deep snowfall.

The lead rider was getting closer and closer, his shadow spreading over me. I could feel myself slowing down in the cruel heat and I could hear the grunts and groans of his horse. He rode up beside me and took a deadly swipe at my head. I felt a swish of air pass through my hair as I ducked just in time. He then reached for my shirt which he grabbed but then let go, causing me to trip, falling face first into the sand. I slowly raised my head and spit sand out of my mouth. I cleared my eyes and could see that the rider had turned his horse around and was heading back towards me. Behind me, the three others had arrived. I was doomed.

I tried to stand up and run, but the lead rider lashed out at me with a whip, binding my legs together. I fell back down and lay in the hot sand staring up at him. "Run all you want, but as you can see, there is nowhere to hide!" He was right.

"Please, let me go! I can explain!" I yelled in total fear.

He stared at me with his dark eyes, lowering the covering from his face to reveal an evil grin that displayed his brown, jagged and decaying teeth. In a deep coarse voice he screamed, "SILENCE!"

He grabbed the collar of my shirt and dragged me through the sand to the rear of a crate which they had been towing. Then he let me go and I fell back into the sand. His men grabbed me from the desert floor, picked me up and hoisted me into the crate headfirst. They slammed the door and locked it. I was trapped.

2

Room For One More

UGGHH! I landed on my stomach, my hands shielding my face as I skidded to the back of the crate. I lay for a moment, stunned and exhausted. What had just happened? I hadn't even had a chance to get my bearings and I was already in some serious trouble. It was dark and my eyes took a while to adjust, but when they did, I noticed that the crate was actually a wooden cage on top of a cart, loosely draped with a sheet and big enough for the three of us. THREE OF US! I found myself looking into the fearful eyes of two others, a boy and a girl, both of whom were about my age. From the looks on their faces, it was clear that this was not a good place to be.

"Are you all right?" asked the boy quietly, trying not to draw the attention of our captors. I was still confused and pretty scared. I hadn't expected to be caged within minutes of arriving in who-knows-where. I sat and stared at them as they stared back at me. They looked very strange to me, and to them, I probably looked like someone who had just parked his spaceship outside. The two were both dressed in white robes and each had very unusual but matching hairstyles. Their heads were almost shaven, except for a braid of hair which grew on one side, and hung down to their shoulders. They were both about my size, and had very dark eyes.

"Are you all right?" repeated the boy.

"Yes, I think so," I said, sounding really confused while carefully examining my new surroundings.

"My name is Ghamen and this is my sister Mayza. What is your name?"

"My name . . . um . . . oh, my name." Wow, in all this craziness I had almost forgotten my name. "My name is Tommy, Tommy T. Timson." Of course!

I then fired off a stream of questions. "What's going on here? Who are these guys? Why are we in this cage?" I was becoming more and more comfortable with asking questions in strange places. Mayza and Ghamen became very quiet and withdrawn. I wasn't sure if I had been too fast with my questions or if they were afraid to talk about how they had landed in this cage.

Mayza finally spoke up, saying something about their parents, but was quickly cut off by Ghamen who said, "These men are very bad. They are tomb raiders and have captured us because we are small." Mayza then spoke up again.

"But Ghamen? Our parents? Maybe he can help?"

Ghamen glared at Mayza and continued with his story. "The **tombs** they raid often have very narrow tunnels that they cannot fit into because of their size. They will use us to crawl into the tunnels to steal treasures for them."

I wasn't sure what was going on with these two, but it was clear that they weren't telling me everything and it was starting to make me uncomfortable.

"Well, we have to get out of here," I said under my breath, parting the sheets that draped the cage to get a better view of the landscape. I still didn't know where I was and now I had to figure out a way to escape from these tomb raiders.

Where was Percival anyway? Had he abandoned me? This was crazy! Even though I knew he was magical, I was doubtful that he'd ever be able to find me in here. Everything was really wrong and I had no idea how I was going to fix it.

I continued to stare out into the desert, hoping to figure out where I was, or maybe even to spot Percival, but what I saw really surprised me. Not far off was a river that stretched as far as I could see. Green fields grew on either side and although I was pretty far away, I could see people working in the distance. I kept scanning the landscape for more clues. Further away stood the triangular structures I had noticed when I first dropped in. There were actually three of them and I could now see that they were **pyramids**.

For a minute, I had thought that maybe I had landed in Egypt, but I had never heard of a river or green fields in Egypt. I was surprised that I hadn't noticed any of this while I was on foot. Maybe I'd seen it, but I was so preoccupied with what had happened to me, that it hadn't registered in my head.

Hours passed, and the convoy continued to move slowly through the sand, the cage bobbing and swaying up and down, side to side. It was cooler in the cage under the protection of the sheet. There wasn't much to say, so the three of us sat quietly doing our own thing. Ghamen was playing with the wooden bars, staring at the wheels of the crate through a crack in the floor. Mayza had her eyes closed and was sitting with her head against the cage. I lay on my back, staring at the roof, thinking about the mess I was in. After a while, I sat up and asked, "Where are they taking us?" I didn't know where I was and I hoped that their answer would give me a clue.

"They are taking us to the **Valley of the Kings**," Ghamen explained.

"The valley of the who?" I asked.

"The Valley of the Kings, you know, in Upper Egypt near the town of **Thebes**."

"Oh yeah, that valley. Sorry, it's been a long day," I said, trying to hide the fact that I had no idea what he was talking about, although now at least I knew I was in Egypt. WOW, Egypt! "Is that where the tombs are?" I continued.

"Yes," replied Mayza. Her answer was short because I think she assumed I knew more about the place than I really did. I had to start asking more questions to learn what was going on. I had to know more if I was going to get out of this mess.

"So what's so special about this Valley of the Kings anyway?" I asked bluntly.

The two smiled and looked at each other, and then Ghamen spoke. "You are not from around here, are you?"

I smiled back and replied, "No, not exactly."

"Where are you from?" asked Mayza.

I decided not to play dumb and use the same 'bump on the head' excuse that I had used with the knights back in England. Besides, it was too dark in the cage to notice my bump, and how would I even know I had lost my memory without someone else bringing up the possibility? I mean, I wouldn't know if I had lost my memory because I wouldn't remember losing it! Right?

I replied, "I'm from very far away."

"Hmmm," responded Ghamen. For some reason, my answer seemed to satisfy the two of them, which satisfied me.

"So tell me about this Valley of the Kings," I continued.

"The Valley is home to the tombs of many kings," explained Ghamen. "Over hundreds of years, many of the great kings of Egypt, following the lead of King Thutmosis I, have had their tombs built there, so that when they die they will have a place to be buried next to other kings. The priests bury them with their valuable possessions that they will need in the afterlife and it is these treasures that the thieves are after."

"How long will it take to get there?" I asked.

"The Valley is very far from here. It will take us many, many days," Ghamen replied sadly.

Many Days! I didn't have many days. I had one day and one day only! I had to get out of here and fast. I needed to find Percival and get the key to my next magical door. If I didn't escape from here soon, I'd never get home! Turning away from them, I reached into my pocket and took a peek at my watch. It was already 6:30 pm! I started to panic. "We have to get out of here! We have to escape!" I said frantically.

"There is no way to escape; soon we will be far from the **Nile** and in the middle of the desert. If we try to escape then, we will surely die of thirst and exposure," answered Ghamen, with a hopeless look on his face.

I assumed the Nile had something to do with the river and the fields, but I wasn't about to ask and lose my train of thought. "There has to be a way! There's always a way!" I said in a determined voice, starting to panic even more as I felt around the cage for an opening or a weakness. To my dismay, the cage was very sturdy. "How long have the two of you been held captive?"

"Three days," answered Ghamen, as he put his arm around his sister to comfort her. The two of them sat quietly, holding each other tight.

"Do they ever let you out?"

"Yes. Every evening they stop to eat and take shelter for the night. They let us out to do the dirty work and then we are thrown back in with scraps of food from their meal," replied Mayza, with a tear slowly trickling down her cheek.

"Well, that's our only chance. When do you think they will stop next?" I asked, and just as I finished my sentence, the cart came to a halt. My heart skipped a beat as the three of us turned and stared at each other.

Ghamen gulped and said, "I think they just have."

3

Taking Care Of Business

The cage was completely still and we were afraid to say anything, but after a few moments I freaked out and asked aloud, "What's going on?"

"QUIET IN THERE! NOT A WORD!" a voice commanded from outside, as we jumped with fright. I was sorry I had opened my big mouth.

Mayza turned to her brother and whispered, "Oh Ghamen, I can't go through another night of this." She was trembling, hiding her face against her brother's shoulder. Ghamen tried to reassure her, but he didn't look so sure himself.

"What's going on?" I repeated, this time in a soft whisper.

Quietly, Ghamen slid closer to me and whispered in my ear, "We have stopped for the night. These nightly stops are horrible. Soon this peace and quiet will be over and we will be put to work," he said, his face twisted with fear.

He turned back to his sister to comfort her and as he placed his arm around her shoulder, a racket began at the door of the cage. A wooden lever was suddenly lifted and the doors opened. We were finally being let out, but to what? Ghamen made his way to the opening and jumped down onto the sand, followed by his sister.

I hung back in the shadows for a moment, but when one of the men peered inside, I decided to move, and fast! I was greeted by the thief who earlier had turned my underwear into a sandbox by dragging me along the desert floor. The man was shorter than I had thought. His skin was like old leather, beaten by the wind and scarred from the desert sun. His nose was crooked, as if it had been kicked by one of his horses, and his hair was jet black, short and straight.

"We did not stop for you to put your feet up and relax," he snarled, clearing his throat, "so DON'T let me catch you resting." He looked me in the eyes and I nodded nervously.

I jumped down from the box and landed in the soft sand. The glare of the sun was gone, which made it easier for me to see. To my surprise, the sky was now a deeper shade of blue, almost purple. The hours were passing quickly and time was getting short. The three of us stood facing the ill-tempered leader of the gang, who had not taken a liking to me at all. To the right of us, his accomplices were tending to the animals, six horses, each in varying shades of brown.

He then gave us our orders. "We will be setting up camp here for the night. You!" he said, pointing to Ghamen, "You will be tending the fire tonight!" He grabbed Ghamen's head roughly and turned it towards a pile of wood they had brought along with their supplies.

"You!" he said, pointing to Mayza. "You will be cooking the food tonight. For your sake, don't let anything burn!" Then he said, pounding his index finger into my chest, "A special job for you, my little friend. You will be tending our animals."

Animals? That can't be too bad. I like animals.

Ghamen and Mayza were told to unload the food and sleeping gear, while I was handed a brush and a shovel. "What's the shovel for?" I asked, thinking they had given it to me by mistake.

"It is for all the manure you will be burying. That is unless you would prefer to use your bare hands!" he said, as the three thieves laughed wickedly.

I squeezed the shovel as my eyes focused on the back ends of the six large horses, their tails swaying in the air. UGH! Dad had always said, "Tommy, sometimes in life, we end up with the short end of the stick." I definitely had the short end this time! With a brush in one hand and a shovel in the other, I had officially become Tommy the Human Pooper Scooper.

From where I was working, I could see everything. Directly in front of the cage was an open patch of sand where their equipment was laid out, followed by an area where, presumably, they would sleep and a fire pit which the thieves had dug carefully. While I worked, I looked up once in a while to watch my two companions, finally understanding why Mayza feared these nightly stops.

The thieves surrounded her and were treating her like a slave. They were gathered around the fire and I watched as one of the men rubbed a piece of bread in the ground and yelled, "You served me this with sand all over it! Clean it off!" The other men laughed aloud as he threw it at her.

Another yelled, "Get me more food! I'm still hungry!" She was very busy, feeding the men bread, fruit and some kind of stew that was cooking over the fire. They were also gulping down a strange drink and I was getting hungry just watching them.

From what I could see, Ghamen was also being treated poorly. Every time the fire faded, he was yelled at and he constantly made trips to get more wood. Often he would fall carrying wood to the pit and the men would laugh and tease him. His courage was impressive as he ignored the remarks and kept moving.

As for me, I was up to my knees in . . . actually, for your sake I won't even say it!

The evening was endless and I continued with my animal-related chores. Mayza and Ghamen were given new tasks. They had to put some kind of ointment on the men's feet. I didn't know what was worse: anointing sweaty feet or, well . . . shovelling horse poop!

The three of us worked throughout the evening while the four men relaxed. The moon and stars were now shining high above, and the landscape had been covered by darkness. Around the fire, conversation continued among the men, who acted as though we weren't even there.

"This trip is taking too long. We should travel at night. The heat is unbearable and we are running out of supplies!" exclaimed one of the thieves.

A second jumped in, "No! Night travel is too dangerous. It is dark and we will never find our way. I think we should . . ."

A third man with very thin cheekbones interrupted, and an argument broke out. They argued about the route and the destination, but I noticed that the leader had not said a word, only glancing back and forth at them, shaking his head. I watched him slowly stand up and draw a deep breath.

"SILENCE!" he yelled.

The thieves quickly became quiet, and only the crackling of the fire could be heard. He then spoke in a deep, angry voice.

"Do you forget what type of journey we are on? This was never meant to be fun. We left our home in **Sais** many days ago and are on a journey that may be the LAST we ever take. This journey will lead us to the city of Thebes, home to the Valley of the Kings, the resting place of the greatest rulers of our time! There will find treasures, enough to make us all rich beyond our wildest dreams."

The three men sat silently, hanging on his every word.

"We have been travelling south through this low desert for many days now. Our sources have assured us that the tomb we are searching for is untouched, deep within the Valley," he said, pointing to a map that had been laid out in front of them.

Pulling two scrolls from his robe, he continued. "These scrolls show exactly where the opening of the tomb lies. They also provide us with hidden routes that lead in and out of the Valley of the Kings. I suggest you study them carefully!" The leader tossed the scrolls to his men and stood up. He then walked over to me, pulled me by the arm and dragged me back to the cage. Without hesitation this time, I got in and crawled to the back. After he left, I inched my way to an opening and peered out, curious to see what would happen next. Mayza and Ghamen sat motionless on the desert floor.

"Both of you! Get out of my sight!" one of the robbers yelled, causing Mayza and Ghamen to hurry to the cage and hop inside. Two of the gang stood up, stepped over the map and proceeded to the sleeping mats, leaving the last one to sit alone. The lone thief looked at the scrolls and examined them carefully. After many minutes, he rolled them up, grabbed the map and made his way to the sleeping area. Before settling, he quickly turned back to the three of us and threw the leftover food in the cage. SLAM! The door of the cage was shut and the lever was dropped, leaving us sitting in the dark.

Outside, all was quiet, save for the soft crackle of the fire that was slowly dying. Inside the cage, both Ghamen and Mayza were crying. I couldn't believe that this had been their third night in this terrible box. I wanted to say something to comfort them, but I couldn't think of anything good, so I just pushed the food towards them and we slowly began to eat. We ate in silence while Ghamen and Mayza wiped the tears from their faces, our stomachs aching from hunger. There was not much food but we shared it evenly.

Following our pathetic meal, Mayza and Ghamen wished me goodnight, lay down on the hard floor, and within minutes were asleep. I couldn't blame them. I, however, found it difficult to sleep in my new quarters.

Except for an occasional snort from the horses, everything was quiet. Resting on my knees, I held onto the wooden bars and looked up at the moon through a crack in the covering. What a day it had been! I could see the shapes of the thieves sleeping quietly beside the glow of the fire and I could see my watch lying in the sand. MY WATCH! SAND! NO! Just when I thought things couldn't get any worse, they did. What was I going to do? I stared at my watch in disbelief as time slowly slipped away.

4

Sweet Dreams

A cool breeze swept in through the sheets that draped our cage. It was colder than I ever thought a desert could be. I pulled my collar tight and zipped my coat all the way up. I looked over and found my new friends, now fast asleep. The cold wind didn't seem to bother them at all. Poor Mayza and Ghamen had already endured three long days at the hands of these thieves and it didn't look as though we'd be free any time soon. I looked up at the sky and saw more stars than I ever knew existed. I felt completely helpless and to make matters worse, I didn't know the time or how I was supposed to find Percival. What kind of wizard was he anyway if he'd let me end up here? This wasn't fair! I land in Egypt, I don't even have a chance to take a breath and then I end up in this stupid cage!

I felt scared and frustrated and I started to think of my family. They must be worried sick. It felt like I'd been gone forever. My poor mom, she must be going crazy, and my dad and even Tina. I should have tried to escape while I was taking care of the horses.

I continued staring at the stars, my mind exhausted. Looking out into space soothed me, and for a moment, I felt at peace. My mind slowed and I started wondering about the girl who was also lost in time. I doubted that she was in this much trouble and I wondered where she was and whom she'd met. I realized I knew absolutely nothing about her. I didn't know what she looked liked or how she talked or anything. I was sure she was nice, but you never know what time travel can do to a person. I wondered if she was enjoying her journey, unlike me. Had Percival had a chance to tell her a bit about me? Not that it mattered now. It wasn't like I'd be seeing him or her anytime soon.

I thought about writing my pen pal a letter and then sighed softly, "What's the point?" What am I going to say? 'Dear Anna, I'm lost in time, I'm in Egypt. I was hoping to meet you but I've been captured by thieves because I'm small. Now I'm not going to be able to meet Percival, my wizard friend, so that he can give me a magical key which opens a magical door.' Right, like she'd believe that! I sighed in disbelief. How could this be happening to me?

A breeze caught the left side of my face and slapped the fear back into me. My gut tensed and my mind raced. I felt nauseous and for a moment I thought I might be sick all over Mayza and Ghamen, so I took a few deep breaths to regain control. The deep breaths relieved my sickness but I still felt anxious and scared. I struggled to my knees and started to panic, grabbing hold of the bars and shaking them with all my strength. Come on! BREAK! I kept shaking until I collapsed and began to sob uncontrollably. Mayza and Ghamen had somehow remained asleep throughout my fit and I didn't want to wake them and have them see me like this. I lay down exhausted and continued to cry, my head resting in my arms. I'll never get home! I'll never see my family again! Why did this have to happen to me? So much was running through my mind. I was so overwhelmed with fear and desperation, that at one point I thought I might never sleep again. Eventually, however, I did and soon the three of us were fast asleep, nuzzled together in our new home.

"Tommy, Tommy, wake up, it's time to get up."

"Mmpphh . . ."

"Wake up, Tommy, wake up."

"Mmpphh . . . . Where am I?"

"You're someplace safe."

"What?" I rubbed the sleep out of my eyes and slowly awoke. My eyes gradually focused and I found myself looking up at a girl who was no older than I was. She had blonde hair that fell to her shoulders and soft green eyes that sparkled in the sunlight. She was dressed in a yellow sundress with white sandals on her feet and a silver necklace that hung around her neck. She was smiling and offered me her hand, which I took. She helped me up and because I was still feeling sleepy, I stretched my arms to the sky. The sun was shining and the breeze was warm against my skin. We were standing in a grassy field which bordered a small pond, where oak and willow trees were scattered here and there. I felt very comfortable.

"Come on," she said.

"Where are we going?" I asked.

"Follow me," she said, offering her hand once again.

I took it and she led me down a narrow path to the water's edge. Under a weeping willow tree lay an old log that made for a perfect bench. She led me to it and we sat down and looked out onto the water. It was perfectly still, except for a duck to our right, which occasionally dipped its beak. It was peaceful and I felt comfortable sitting there. The girl picked up a stone and casually threw it into the pond.

"How did you sleep?" she asked.

"Well," I replied.

"I thought you'd never wake up," she said with a smile, tossing another stone into the water.

"It's really nice here," I said, also picking up a stone and throwing it in the pond.

"This is my favourite place to come. I love the willow trees and the water," she said, looking around, obviously very happy to be where she was. She was very beautiful and looked as though she didn't have a care in the world. She sat quietly and stared out at the water, nibbling her lower lip and gently tapping a finger against her knee. She was completely at ease and it felt good to be sitting with her.

"Do you live around here?" I asked, looking around for another stone to throw.

"No, I just like to come here and watch the ducks and the birds," she said, pointing to a branch high up in an oak tree to our right. "See that one. I've named him James. He visits me whenever I come here."

"Hello, James," I said, waving to the bird that sat in the tree.

"James likes to eat berries and sing me songs."

"What songs does he sing?" I asked.

"He sings all my favourite songs, but I don't think he'll sing today."

"Do you know that one?" I asked, pointing to a small sparrow that sat on a rock not far from us.

"No I don't. I've never seen him before. Let's name him together."

"Alright, how about we name him Sandy?" I suggested.

"Sandy the sparrow," she said, carefully reviewing it in her mind. "Sandy it is. Hello Mr. Sandy," she said making it official.

"Hello, Sandy," I followed, greeting our new friend.

We sat in silence comfortably enjoying each other. She was unlike any one I had ever met before and we shared a close connection that I couldn't put my finger on. She began to hum and leisurely look for small stones to toss into the pond. After a few moments, I noticed a dark grey cat climbing in the tree directly overhead. I was surprised that I hadn't seen it before, since I'd apparently been sitting right under it. The two of us sat quietly, admiring the agility of the cat as it crept onto a small branch that reached far out over the water.

"I wonder what it's trying to do. There's nothing on the end of that branch," I exclaimed.

"Maybe he just wants to see how far he can go," she responded.

"Maybe," I added, when all of a sudden the branch broke, sending the animal plunging into the pond.

"Oh no!" I said, jumping up from the log. "It's going to drown!" The girl leaped up after me and grabbed my arm.

"No, he's fine. Look! He's starting to swim," she said, trying to comfort me.

"It's drowning! It can barely keep its head above water!" I yelled. It was awful to watch the struggling cat disappear repeatedly under the water only to resurface later. It moved so slowly that I didn't think it had any chance at all.

"Just give him a chance; I know he can make it," she said soothingly.

"I don't care! I'm going in after it," I said, moving towards the water.

"No, you can't. You have to let him do this on his own," she said calmly, as she held onto my arm.

I watched helplessly as the cat struggled for its life, slowly inching its way through the water. It seemed like an eternity. I looked at the girl, who had lessened her grip on my arm. She watched with a smile, whispering words of encouragement to the poor cat. Finally, one of the longest minutes of my life passed and the cat, exhausted, emerged safe but wet from the pond. It walked towards us but stopped just short and began to lick itself clean.

"Thank goodness," I stated, as I sat myself back down on the log and rested my head in my hands. "That was awful. I can't believe you didn't want to help it," I continued.

The girl sat down next to me and said, "He didn't need our help. He did just fine."

"Well, what if he had drowned? Then how would you have felt?" I asked.

"If I had thought he was going to drown, I would have sent you in after him."

"I don't know. I'm just glad it's over," I said, watching the cat nestle against the girl's leg.

"That wasn't so bad, was it, Ray," she said to the cat, as she stroked it gently.

"Who's Ray?" I asked.

"The cat, silly," she said with a smile, as she gently picked it up.

"Ray? I don't know if I'd name a cat Ray."

"You see, Tommy," she continued, "now he knows how to swim and he also knows not to walk on small branches."

"And that he hates water," I added.

"Maybe, but he's still better off now for having experienced that, and for not having given up."

"I still think we should have helped him," I said.

"Sometimes we need help, but often we just think we need help. It's important that we learn the difference, because most things can be accomplished if we don't give up and just try our best, just like Ray," she explained, proudly looking at her cat.

I turned back toward the water thinking about what had just happened, when she stood up and said, "Ray and I have to go, but it was really nice spending time with you."

"It was nice spending time with you, too," I responded.

"Good-bye," she said, as she turned and walked away with Ray in her arms.

I slowly turned to face the pond, but suddenly jumped to my feet. "Wait!" I shouted, but she was gone. I had realized that I'd not even learned her name.

"Ugh." I awoke suddenly to find myself lying on the floor of the cage. It was still dark and Mayza and Ghamen were still fast asleep. Had I been dreaming? The slow realization that it was all just a dream was shocking. It had all seemed so real: the pond, the cat, the girl. For a moment, I longed to be back there; to sit under the willow tree with her and toss stones into the pond. I looked around, and through the sheet that draped us, saw that the sky was beginning to brighten. I thought back to my dream and remembered what she had said about not giving up. I knew I had to act fast. Our captors would soon be up, and then there would be no chance of escape. I decided at that moment that there was no way I'd ever let these thieves keep me from seeing my family and as long as I still had time, I was determined that I would make it. Check out time had arrived!

5

The Cradle Will Rock

I sat quietly, staring at Ghamen and Mayza. The sky was just starting to lighten, so I assumed that it was really early in the morning. I sat listening for any sounds, but the only thing I could hear was the wind. I took a peek through the sheet and could barely make out the shapes of the thieves. They were still asleep. The wind had really picked up and I was surprised that they were able to sleep through it. If I was going to escape, it had to be soon. I looked around for my watch but couldn't see it. The wind must have blown sand over it. I had an idea where it might be and knew that as soon as I was out of the cage, I'd have to go digging for it.

Mayza and Ghamen were still asleep. They lay snuggled together in a corner of the cage. I hated waking people up, but if we were going to get out of here, we all had to help. I nudged them, "Hey guys, we have to get up." I poked them harder but they still wouldn't wake up. Give me a break! I'm locked in a cage with the two soundest sleepers in the world–just my luck! I noticed that they were both breathing through their noses, which I decided to plug. I figured that when the two stopped breathing, they would wake up. Well, they stopped breathing all right, but after some time, I was still holding their noses and they were still not breathing! Then I got scared and thought I had killed them! I let go of their noses and they started breathing again which made me feel a whole lot better, except they were still asleep. So I licked my two index fingers and put them in their ears. Rich, the school bully had introduced me to this. I hated it, and was so glad that I wasn't on the receiving end of it this time. I really moved my fingers around so that I'd get the insides of their ears all wet. They finally started squirming and moaning and soon after, woke up. I took my fingers back quickly so they wouldn't know what I'd just done.

"Hey, we have to get up," I said again softly.

"What is happening?" Ghamen said sleepily.

"It's time to get out of here. We have to leave now!" I said, turning to Mayza, who was still rubbing her eyes.

"You think we can escape?" Ghamen asked, staring at the floor. He was still pretty tired.

"We have to escape and NOW's our only chance," I said, becoming impatient with my tired friends. I hadn't thought it was going to be this difficult to get them going. After all, it was their third night in this miserable cage. "Listen," I continued, "the thieves are still sleeping and between the three of us, we should be able to figure this out. There's got to be a way out of here!"

"What did you have in mind?" asked Mayza, who was starting to come around.

"I haven't got that far yet. Waking you guys up took most of my imagination."

"Look outside," said Ghamen. "The wind has really picked up," he stated, as a gust hit us all in the face. "Wow! That was strong enough to blow us over!" I exclaimed.

"That's it!" Mayza cried out in excitement.

"What's it?" I asked.

"Blowing us over," she said.

"What do you mean?" I asked.

"I am confused," added Ghamen.

"So am I," I said.

"Yeah, I'm really confused," Ghamen said again.

"Listen!" Mayza said impatiently. "Blowing us over! If we could knock the cage over, it might break," she explained.

Ghamen and I looked at each other in silence and then looked back at Mayza who had a big smile on her face. "I think that could work," I said.

"We would all have to lean on one side and slowly rock the cage together," Mayza said, continuing with her explanation.

"We could get hurt," said Ghamen, who didn't look too thrilled about the plan.

"You always worry about hurting yourself," complained Mayza. "If we are careful when we fall, we will all be fine."

"It sounds good to me," I said, "but we have to do this now. The wind is really starting to blow and those thieves will wake up soon."

"All right then, let's rock it from this side, away from where they are sleeping," Ghamen said, taking a deep breath.

The three of us moved to one side of the cage and slowly began rocking it. We all had to rock at the same time, so Mayza set the rhythm. ". . . and rock, and rock, and rock . . . ." Soon, the cage started to lift to one side. Mayza's plan was working and the wind was loud enough to muffle the banging that the cage made each time it rocked. The more we rocked, the closer we came to spilling the cage over the edge of the cart. I looked at Ghamen who closed his eyes tight every time we tipped the cage. I think Ghamen was really afraid, but I could tell Mayza loved all of this. She looked very serious as she continued giving the orders to rock. I was excited to be finally trying to escape, although I did share Ghamen's concerns about actually falling to the ground. I mean, I'm not afraid of heights or anything, but I don't often launch myself off the side of a cart, especially while in a cage.

It took a couple of minutes, but we soon had a nice rhythm going and all of a sudden, "WHOOOOAAAA!" The cage fell off the side of the cart and THUD–we landed hard in the sand.

"Is everyone all right?" asked Mayza.

"I think so," responded Ghamen.

"I'm okay," I said.

"Did it break?" asked Ghamen.

"I don't know," I said, as I started looking for damage.

"Look here!" Mayza said, pointing to one side of the cage where all the wooden bars had caved in.

"Perfect, that's all we need! Come on, let's start pulling them apart," I said excitedly. We frantically kicked and pushed the wooden bars apart.

"It's working!" exclaimed Ghamen with a smile–the first smile I'd seen on him since we'd met.

"I think I can squeeze out," Mayza said, twisting her way through the broken bars. "I'm out!"

"Ghamen, you're next. Let's go, we have to hurry," I said, anxiously coaxing him through the hole we had made.

"I'm out. Come on, Tommy, hurry! I think they're waking up!" Ghamen said nervously.

Once we were all out, we hid behind the cart. The wind was getting stronger and the sand was now blowing all around us. The sounds of the storm were making it hard to hear, so we had to start raising our voices. At the same time we had to make sure the thieves hadn't noticed anything, so Ghamen peered around the cart, "They are still sleeping. I think I can do it."

"Think you can do what?" I asked, not knowing what he meant.

"I think I can get the scrolls!" Ghamen replied.

"Are you crazy? Let them keep the scrolls! We're free. Let's get out of here!" I hollered at him, while turning to Mayza for support, but before she could speak he was gone. I peered around the broken cart and watched him dash off to where the thieves were sleeping. I knew I

33

couldn't let him go alone so I chased after him. I took a few steps, and then quickly remembered that my watch was still lost, so I headed to where I thought I had dropped it. I looked for it but I could hardly see a thing as the blowing sand stung my face. I dropped to my knees and started feeling around, but I couldn't find it.

I was facing the thieves and looked up to see if they were awake. I knew it was only a matter of minutes and maybe even seconds before they would wake, because nobody could sleep in this storm. I noticed Ghamen moving sneakily around the site. He was searching furiously through the bags that lay beside the thieves. I held my breath and watched him closely, when suddenly one of them began to wake up. I panicked and froze in the sand. The thief sat up but he was still half asleep and didn't notice anything. Ghamen continued to rifle through the bags, unaware of the danger behind him. Finally, I saw him holding something in his hands, but suddenly a huge gust of wind blew sand everywhere, causing him to disappear. All I could do was cover my face and head back in the direction of the cage.

"Tommy! Over here!" It was Mayza, and I followed her voice. Her face was partially covered by her robe.

"I don't know where your brother is! I think he got lost in the storm!"

"We can't leave him! I'm going to look for him!" Mayza yelled, through the noise of the wind.

"No! It's too dangerous! The thieves are awake!" I shouted back.

"We have to help him. If they find him it will be all over for him!"

"All right! I'll search for him! Stay right here!" I said, turning around, coming face to face with Ghamen.

"Tommy, I'm right here!" said Ghamen, proudly showing off the scrolls in his hands.

"You scared us half to death! Are you crazy?" I shouted.

"I had to get the scrolls!"

"You could have been caught!" I yelled.

"But I didn't get caught! Here put these in your bag!" Ghamen shouted, handing me the scrolls. "Quickly, we must head for the Nile. We can get help there," he explained.

"Cover your face with your shirt, Tommy," Mayza said. "It will help protect you from the sand."

"Okay, now let's get out of here!" I shouted, as I hurriedly placed the scrolls in my backpack.

"Stay low and follow me. Make sure you stay right behind me so that the storm will cover our tracks," Ghamen shouted back at us.

I took one last look back in hopes of seeing my watch, but it wasn't there. It was gone for good. I looked over and noticed that the thieves were all awake and scrambling to keep their belongings from blowing away.

"I think they're on to us. Let's get going!" I said to Ghamen.

"Okay, let's go!" replied Ghamen, as he started out into the desert with Mayza and me following closely behind.

6

Family Secrets

We moved slowly through the storm and I kept glancing back to make sure we were still alone, but the sand was blowing so fiercely that I couldn't see anything. I wasn't sure how quickly the thieves would notice we were gone, but I was sure it wouldn't be long. Ghamen and Mayza had pulled their robes over their faces to protect them from the storm and I had my jacket wrapped around my head as the three of us staggered along in single file, hoping that the storm would soon end. Then maybe we could get some kind of idea of where we were headed.

"Do you think they are following us?" Ghamen yelled through the heavy winds.

"I don't know! The storm is really bad!" I shouted.

"Of course they're after us! We have the scrolls!" Mayza exclaimed.

We continued to move through the desert, over mounds of sand that continually shifted and changed shape in the wind. We were tired and would often stumble and fall, but we worked as a team to keep each other going. We all knew we had to make it out of this storm no matter how difficult the trek was going to be, and although we didn't know where we were going, we had to keep moving.

My legs were tired and my whole body ached. We were walking for what seemed like days, and just when I thought we'd never make it, the storm began to clear. It was unreal how quickly it faded. One minute we were engulfed in a sandstorm and the next we were safe. The three of us turned to look back and could see the storm, like a swarm of bees, violently heading out deep into the desert.

"Holy cow! Can you believe that?" I said excitedly.

"Holy cow? Nobody says that anymore," exclaimed Mayza, rolling her eyes.

"The storm just cleared!" I stated, beaming with joy.

"We were lucky. I've often heard of people wandering into the desert and never being seen again. Sandstorms are very unforgiving," Ghamen explained.

"Does anybody know where we are?" I asked, scanning the horizon that was brightening.

"It's difficult to tell. We could be anywhere," Ghamen said, also looking around. "Let's climb that crest," he continued. "Maybe we will be able to see something familiar."

The three of us crawled up the steep sand dune. It was the biggest one I had seen yet and I was sure that we'd be able to see pretty far, once we made it to the top. Again I found myself following the others; I couldn't believe how fast they could climb the dunes. I chased after them and met them at the peak. I was totally exhausted and stood curled over, resting my palms on my knees, panting heavily, trying to regain my breath. I looked up at Ghamen and Mayza. "I'm okay," I said, raising my hand and gasping for air.

"You look terrible," Mayza said, trying to hold back her laughter.

"I'm just not used to running up these dunes," I said, breathing heavily.

"You won't have to deal with them much longer," Ghamen said with a smile, looking out over the two of us. Mayza and I who were facing Ghamen slowly turned around.

"Look!" I yelled.

The three of us stared with open mouths at an amazing array of green colours in the near distance. "Wow! Look at that! We made it!" Mayza shouted with excitement.

"We did! We made it!" sighed Ghamen, reaching out to hug his sister.

"Where are we?" I asked, equally excited but a little confused.

"That's the Nile, Tommy! Come on, let's hurry!" cried Ghamen.

We ran as fast as we could towards the green valley ahead of us, taking short quick steps through the sand. I still couldn't believe my eyes. Up ahead was nothing I had ever imagined Egypt to be. It was green everywhere and water seemed to stretch out forever. We ran until we were close enough to make everything out and then, out of breath, we slowed almost to a halt.

"Mayza, I know this area!" Ghamen said panting, while pointing to a large mound of sand and stone. "A branch of the Nile is just over there! It is . . ."

"Branch of the Nile? What are you talking about Ghamen?" Mayza interrupted.

"Let me finish, Mayza! Shhh!"

Mayza huffed, crossed her arms and listened. "Brother and sister," I snickered.

"That stream of water is a branch of the Nile. There are many places to hunt here. Father used to take me on trips along this stretch of water. We would spend hours travelling up and down the stream. On one of our journeys, our boat got damaged and we had to repair it. This is where it happened! That mound of sand over there was where we sheltered in the shade to fix the boat." Ghamen smiled, as he talked about his father. "Maybe we can find some help," he continued. "Hunters often pursue their prey in the early morning hours. Come on, follow me."

Mayza and I followed Ghamen towards the place where he and his father had repaired their boat. I was really happy to know that I was finally heading in the right direction, but I still had a lot of things to deal with. My watch was gone and I didn't have any idea of what time it was. Percival was nowhere in sight and I was beginning to think that I might never see him again. If that were the case, how was I supposed to find the door, not to mention the key? Ugh, what a mess. I felt like throwing up.

"Ghamen! Tommy's turning green," Mayza said, wearing a worried look.

"I'm all right. I'm just a little winded from all the running. I'll be fine."

"Let's stop here for a moment," Ghamen said, giving me a pat on the back. The three of us stopped for a breather. Ghamen continued to scan the horizon while Mayza stared at the ground.

"I really miss Mother and Father," Mayza said, burrowing her toes into the sand.

"I really miss them too," Ghamen added, taking Mayza by the hand. It was clear that they both missed their parents dearly. I watched as Mayza leaned her head on her brother's shoulder. The bond they shared was very special. They were not only brother and sister, but they were also close friends. It really made me wish that my sister Tina were here. Sure, we had our differences, but she was my sister and I loved her.

"I'm sure they can't wait to see the two of you. They're probably worried sick," I said, finally catching my breath. The two of them just stared in silence as if neither one had heard me speak. "Hey. What's wrong with you guys? You're going home. You should be excited," I continued, trying to get them to smile.

"It's more complicated than that, Tommy," Ghamen said, as he slowly lifted his eyes from the sand. "There's a lot we haven't told you."

"Like what?" I asked, as Ghamen's eyes fell back onto the sand. "Guys? Come on. Tell me," I said, taking a step towards them.

"It's not that simple," Ghamen said, as he slowly shook his head.

"Maybe I can help," I responded.

"I don't think so," Ghamen said.

"If you don't want to tell me, fine, be that way. But I really think that you would feel a lot better if you did. And who knows, I might even be able to help," I said, pacing back and forth across the sand. The two of them remained silent with their heads lowered. I was trying my best to comfort them but it wasn't doing any good. I was frustrated, and felt that after all we'd been through, they owed me an explanation. I raised my arms in defeat. "Well, are you just going to stand there all day or what? If you're not going to tell me then let's just keep going, because I have to be somewhere later this afternoon!" I said, marching away from them.

"Alright! You want to know? I'll tell you! Those thieves that we just escaped from murdered our father four days ago!" Ghamen yelled.

I froze in my tracks, and shivers ran up and down my spine. I had never expected to hear something like that from Ghamen. I didn't know how to react, so I slowly turned around to face him. His eyes were swollen with tears and Mayza was sobbing softly on his shoulder. I didn't know what to say and was relieved when Ghamen finally began to speak again.

"My parents worked for the Pharaoh, **King Rameses II**. They helped protect the scrolls of the ancient kings, ensuring they remained locked in a vault." He paused to swallow and then continued. "Those thieves were acquaintances of our parents. They betrayed them and stole some of the scrolls. They killed our father and then they kidnapped us."

"What about your mother?" I asked, slowly approaching the two of them.

"Our mother is being held in a prison in **Memphis**. The thieves made it look as though our mother was guilty, when in fact she has done nothing," Ghamen said, as he let go of his sister and began to walk towards me. He grabbed the bag from my shoulder, opened it and retrieved the scrolls. "I am taking these back to prove my mother's innocence and to clear her name," he said with determination.

"Let me help you," I said.

"You are already helping us," Mayza said.

"I had no idea that you had been through so much. I'm sorry I was impatient with you. I just thought that maybe I could help." I was starting to get emotional and it took all the strength I had to hold back the tears.

"It's all right," said Mayza, as she leaned in to give me a big hug. I couldn't hold in the tears any longer and started to howl all over Mayza's shoulder.

"WHAAA!"

"It's okay, Tommy," said Ghamen. "We are going to be all right."

"I'm sorry," I said, continuing to weep. "I just feel so bad about everything."

"Now, now, Tommy," Mayza said, stroking my head. "We'll get through this."

"Sure we will, Tommy," Ghamen said. "Look. I mean, we are free aren't we?"

"Yes," I said, as my sobs slowed.

"And soon we will all be home," Ghamen continued.

"Yeah," I said, as I lifted my head from Mayza's shoulder.

"That's it, Tommy, show me a smile," Mayza said, as she wiped the tears from my eyes.

"See, things aren't that bad," Ghamen said, rubbing my shoulder.

"Let's get those scrolls back to Memphis," I said, sniffling and rubbing my eyes.

"That's what we'll do," said Mayza.

"Yeah, okay," I said.

"Do you feel better?" Ghamen asked.

"Yeah. Do you?" I asked.

"Yes, a little. I'm glad I told you about all of this," Ghamen said with a smile.

"Me too," said Mayza.

"Me too," I repeated, while taking a deep breath.

"Boys, we'd better keep moving. The thieves are still probably caught in the storm, but as soon as it dies down, they'll come after us. Remember, we still have the scrolls."

We both agreed and the three of us headed for the stream ahead. I was finally getting to know my two companions. They were turning out to be really great people and I was thankful for that. If I was going to have any hope in getting to the magical door, it was friends like these that I'd need.

A whole new world lay in front of us as we moved towards the green landscape. A bird swooped down from behind us and disappeared into the green blanket ahead. Many more birds followed behind, honking loudly. Tall green reeds and wild plants were growing everywhere in the wetland. Behind the thicket of plants and reeds, we could see a stream of water–the one Ghamen had spoken about. Wild ducks were flying all around, and I watched as one dropped out of the sky and plunged into the water.

"Did you see that?" I yelled, pointing to the water. "That bird just fell out of the sky!"

"Look up there," Ghamen said, pointing to another duck. I watched as an object flew through the air and hit its body, causing it to lose control. With its neck cranked back, both the bird and the object fell to the water. "Behind those tall reeds are hunters. They hunt birds with boomerangs," Ghamen explained.

Wow, I always thought it would be cool to have my own boomerang, but my dad would kill me if he ever caught me using it to hunt birds!

Ghamen led us towards the tall reeds ahead. The sand, which I was beginning to hate, was becoming much darker and was no longer dry. It was soaking wet and my shoes were beginning to sink into it. At one point, I lost my left one and almost fell face first trying to get it.

We quietly approached the banks of the Nile so that we wouldn't disturb the hunters. We hid in the denseness of the reeds and looking between them was like peering through your fingers during a scary movie–not that I ever do that. We could see many hunters standing barefoot on long narrow boats. They were wearing white cloth around their waists and used a variety of weapons to hunt with, including boomerangs, large harpoons and huge fishing nets. Ghamen motioned for us to huddle so that we could make a plan. We decided that we needed to get the hunters' attention, so I pointed and whispered, "Look guys, there's a rock over there. We can get their attention on that thing. It's huge!"

The three of us slowly waded through the water that was now waist deep. The mud was thick and made it difficult to walk. It was slowing us down and Mayza and Ghamen dropped a few steps behind. I kept moving because I wasn't about to slow down for anything. I crept up to the rock and stopped in front of it, when suddenly, the water around me started to ripple and bubble and I felt a rumbling noise. The rock started to lift itself out of the water and I heard Mayza yelling behind me.

"THAT'S NOT A ROCK! IT'S A . . . AAAHHHHH!"

7

A Bigger Mouth Than Mine

I fell back into the water and found myself staring into the biggest mouth I had ever seen. Within the dark cavern was a tongue the size of Mayza, lying between two very large teeth. It sloshed around, hitting flaps of skin that hung down from the roof of its mouth. I stared deep into its enormous belly and then the creature's gigantic mouth slammed shut and water flew everywhere, knocking me over. "WOOAAHH!" I jerked my head out of the water and looked back for help, but Ghamen and Mayza were too far behind. I wanted to run to them but I was too frightened to do anything.

"Tommy, over here! RUN! It's going to eat you!" Mayza screamed, as I tried to stand up. I looked into the eyes of the angry beast. It saw I was trapped and moved towards me spraying water from its snout. Its mouth opened with a rumbling roar and its jaws began to bear down on me. I shut my eyes and waited to be swallowed whole. Suddenly I was yanked out of the water and heaved onto a small raft.

Some hunters had heard the commotion and one lifted me to safety while two others scared off the beast. I turned to look for the creature that had almost eaten me, but it had disappeared through the reeds and grass. The raft slowly drifted and came to rest beside Mayza and Ghamen who were standing in the murky waters of the marsh.

"Take my hand," one of the hunters said, as he reached down to pull them up. "It is safer in here." They sat beside me, dripping wet. "You are safe now," the man said, as he waved in the other two hunters, who then returned to the boat.

"Your friend is a little Horus, without a harpoon!" one of the hunters said, pulling himself onto the raft. The three of them laughed aloud as the final man came aboard.

"What are they talking about? Who's Horus?" I whispered to Ghamen.

He laughed, "Don't you know the legend of Horus and Seth?"

"Horus and Seth? No, I don't know that one," I responded.

Ghamen shook his head in disbelief and continued, "Anyway, legend has it that when the evil god Seth turned himself into a hippopotamus, the great god Horus hunted him down with a magical harpoon. That's why he called you Horus."

"So that was a hippopotamus?" I asked.

"It sure was. Have you not heard of that legend before?"

"Sure I have. It must have just slipped my mind. I mean, come on, I was almost swallowed by a hippo!"

We settled into the raft that looked as if it was made from strands of hay tied together, running from bow to stern. It was very small, but we all managed to fit comfortably. Nets full of fish and fowl lay together on the floor next to the hunter's tools. Mayza thanked them for all they had done and then Ghamen introduced us. A broad-shouldered hunter placed a hand on my head and said, "You are very fortunate. A moment later and we would have lost you."

"A moment? That was too close. Thanks a lot," I said.

"What are you and your friends doing out here anyway?" asked the hunter.

I was still in shock from the hippopotamus and my hands were shaking like leaves, and for some reason I just started to babble. "We were captured by thieves and locked in a cage and we had to do all this work and they only fed us scraps but we got the scrolls . . ."

"You must slow down. You are speaking so quickly. I think your friend needs some rest," the hunter said to Ghamen and Mayza.

"Yes," said Mayza, "he is very tired."

"He mentioned some scrolls. What was he talking about?" asked the hunter.

Before anyone could answer, I began to pull a scroll from my bag but stopped when Ghamen elbowed me in the ribs. I looked at him as he stared coldly back at me. He then turned to face the hunter and said, "Scrolls? No, no, they are nothing of importance. We make them ourselves and play with them."

"Hmmm . . . ." the hunter responded, his eyes moving suspiciously from Ghamen to his companions. He looked at them and continued, "We are travelling to Memphis. If that is where you want to go, we will take you."

"Oh yes, Memphis is where we want to go," replied Ghamen nervously.

"Yes, thank you," Mayza added, trying to break the tension that was now weighing heavily on all of us. I knew I was in trouble so I sat still, holding my head in my hands, wishing I were invisible.

The sun was pushing its way up over the horizon and the hunters began to prepare for the journey. The hunter that had heaved me out of the water carefully made his way to the rear of the boat. I watched him balance himself confidently as he walked barefoot along the edge of the raft, grabbing a long wooden oar to steer the small boat. The remaining two positioned themselves along opposite sides of the raft and began to row. I gave a sigh of relief, knowing that I was finally heading out of the desert and was on my way to the city of Memphis, wherever that was.

8

Up A Creek

We travelled along the river for some time, watching everything that was going on around us. There were all sorts of boats and rafts and everybody was hard at work hunting or fishing. Along the banks of the stream, people were cutting tall reeds that they gathered into large bundles and carried on their backs.

"These small boats are really strong. See those men over there. Did you know that they spend hours gathering **papyrus** reeds along the marshes of the Nile to build these things?" Ghamen pointed out. "They also use the papyrus for rope, nets, baskets and paper."

The sun continued to rise brightening the sky. It had to be mid-morning but I wasn't sure, because I didn't have my watch and going back for it now would be like searching for a needle in a papyrus stack. AH-HA! I'm talking like an Egyptian already!

Ghamen talked with one of the hunters while Mayza and I, enjoying the scenery, talked about our friends and families. She told me all about her home and I told her all about my family. It felt like forever since I had talked about them.

"Tommy, do you have a brother?" Mayza asked.

"No, I have a younger sister named Tina," I replied smiling. I'd never been so happy to mention her before.

She smiled and took my hand. "Thank you for all you have done for us. If it weren't for your courage, we'd still be stuck in that awful cage. You have been a blessing to Ghamen and me. We are very thankful." She held my hand for only a few seconds, but it felt much longer. I became shy and looked back towards the water.

"You are turning red," she said giggling. Her eyes glanced from my blushing face to the water below.

The raft came to a stop and the broad-shouldered hunter stepped out. I thought we had arrived in Memphis, but I looked up to see him boarding a much larger boat. "Why are we changing boats?" I asked aloud.

"This branch of the river has ended. We are approaching the wider waters of the Nile," the hunter said in a hoarse voice, as he gathered his belongings.

The three of us boarded the larger boat. It was made almost entirely of wood and we took seats in the middle. In the centre, a wooden mast stood tall, holding a large sail that blew in the wind. While waiting to depart, I noticed the three hunters huddled together, talking quietly while looking at us curiously.

"What's going on over there?" I whispered to Ghamen and Mayza.

Mayza replied, "I don't know, but I have a bad feeling about this."

Ghamen then added, "So do I. Something doesn't seem right."

I sat back and placed my arms behind my head, "It's nothing. I can tell that we are in good hands." The broad-shouldered hunter pulled the raft on board and moved to the rear, grabbing a large wooden oar. The other two men took their places and we all sat tight for our journey down the Nile. With the sail up and the wind at our backs, we were off.

"Wow! There is so much water!" I yelled, as we headed onto the main stream of the Nile.

"Of course, Tommy. It's the season of the Nile!" Ghamen exclaimed, his eyes wide with excitement as we raced down the river. "The levels of the Nile have climbed leaving good floodplains all around. Water is needed for farming, for building, for everything! This year was a perfect year!"

We headed up stream and I peered over the side and saw huge boats, a few transporting large stone structures, some with big sails, and others filled with all sorts of animals. Each boat seemed to have a man who steered and others who worked the sails. I couldn't believe it. Boats, sails and water in Egypt! They never taught me that in school!

I looked around the boat and saw that Mayza and Ghamen were busy watching the water while the hunters were busy steering the boat. I was dying to check out the scrolls and I decided that with everyone busy, maybe I could get away with a quick look. I was itching with excitement and the thought of holding material that was written thousands of years before I was born was too much for me to resist.

I slipped off my seat and knelt down on my knees, low enough so that I could hide what I was doing. I opened my bag and pulled out one of the scrolls to look at it. It was a bit damp, but the writing hadn't smudged. The scroll was written in a language I had never seen before, with little coloured pictures and symbols scattered all over the page.

"What have you got there?" I lifted my head slowly to meet the black eyes of one of the hunters, who stood directly above me, looking down at the scroll. "Let me see that."

I gulped as he bent down and pried it from my hands. The hunter's eyes grew big as he stared intently at it. Ghamen, from out of nowhere, grabbed the scroll back from the hunter and rolled it up while saying, "Ha! We can't lose this! It's better kept in the bag. The game's no good without it." The hunter stared at Ghamen as he rolled up the scroll, put it back in the bag, and then turned his back to sit down as if nothing had happened. The hunter looked curiously at me and then retreated to the back of the boat. I took a deep breath and dropped my head in my hands.

"Tommy! You shouldn't have taken the scrolls from the bag!" Ghamen said, handing it back to me.

"Sorry."

"And you can't talk about them or look at them in front of strangers," he said.

"You're right, I'm sorry," I repeated, feeling terrible.

I looked over at Mayza and grinned awkwardly but she didn't look very pleased with me either. I slipped the bag between my legs and sat quietly staring at the floor of the boat. Ghamen was right. I realized that if we lost the scrolls, Ghamen and Mayza would never see their mother again. Curiosity was getting the better of me on these journeys and it was something that I would have to learn to control. I crossed my arms and held them tight to my chest.

We finally came to rest at a large wooden dock and the hunters began to step off the boat to tie it down while the three of us stood up to leave.

"Hold there!" one of the hunters demanded.

"What's going on?" I whispered to Ghamen, who shrugged his shoulders while Mayza raised her eyebrows. The three of us stood silently, waiting for him to speak. The broad-shouldered hunter leaned over us and said, "There is a price to pay for this trip."

The three of us looked anxiously at each other. A price? They had never mentioned anything about a price before. "But sir, as you can see, we have nothing we can give you," Ghamen replied nervously.

The hunter loomed in on us with his dark beady eyes, pointed at me and said, "Of course you do. We want THAT BAG!"

9

Hunting Season

The broad-shouldered hunter continued to stare into my eyes with his hand outstretched, waiting for my schoolbag, which I was holding at my side. Was this guy nuts? Did he honestly expect me to give him the bag? I mean, it's my bag! I wasn't about to give it to anyone, let alone this guy.

"Umm, I can't give you the bag, but I want you to know that we really appreciate the lift into town," I said, trying to be as calm and polite as I possibly could. The hunter stood silent. I looked at Ghamen and Mayza who both shrugged their shoulders.

The one who had demanded my schoolbag looked up at his two companions who were now standing behind Ghamen and Mayza. A sly grin slowly formed on his face.

"I'm not sure that our little friend here understood me," he said to them, as his friends chuckled. He then turned to me. "You are mistaken. I'm not ASKING you for the bag. I'm TAKING the bag!" he roared, as he lurched out with his hand and grabbed hold of one of the straps.

"Hey! Let go! Ghamen! Help!" I desperately struggled with the hunter, holding onto the other strap with all my might. I looked at Ghamen and Mayza, hoping they would come to my aid, but they were struggling with the other hunters who had grabbed them by the shoulders.

"Let go of my bag!" I screamed, swaying frantically from side to side, trying not to let go of it. The hunter's face turned bright red and he looked angrier than my dad did when he found out who flooded our basement, but hey, I was five years old and I really thought I could turn it into a swimming pool.

"Give me the bag!" the broad-shouldered hunter snarled under his breath. I didn't know how long I could hold it. The hunter was very strong and pretty soon he'd not only have my bag, but he'd probably have my arms too! Then Mayza, who had escaped her attacker, appeared holding one of the smaller oars, waving it madly over her head.

"Let go of him!" she cried, at the top of her lungs. The surprised hunter released his hold on the bag and raised his hands to protect himself from the whirling oar. I jumped out of the way, tripped over a pile of fish, and went flying face first onto the floor of the boat. Mayza jumped over a heap of netting and threw the oar at the hunter. He jolted backwards in an attempt to avoid the oar, but his feet got caught up in the netting that was strewn out all along the floor of the boat. He managed to deflect the oar with his hand but the force of the impact sent him staggering back further towards the edge of the boat. He frantically tried to regain his balance, but to no avail. Then to my amazement, Mayza rushed him, and realizing his instability, ran her shoulder into his midsection, knocking him overboard. I closed my eyes tight, waiting for the splash, but it never came. I looked up at Mayza who now stared back at me, breathing heavily with a look of disbelief on her face. He couldn't have disappeared into thin air, I thought to myself, as I struggled to my feet and rushed to Mayza's side. The two of us slowly peered over the edge. Then Mayza smiled and turned to me, "That should hold him for a while." His feet had remained tangled in the mesh and he was now hanging upside down alongside the boat, his head a few inches from the water.

"Wow! Where did you learn to do that?"

"I have an older brother, remember?" she said, as she winked at me with a smile. "Hurry! We have to help Ghamen," she responded without hesitation. I turned around and saw that Ghamen was struggling with the other two hunters. Mayza and I carefully but quickly made our way to the front of the cluttered boat. I wasn't sure how I was going to help him. I had never been in a real fight before and I certainly didn't want to start off with two full-grown, crazy Egyptian hunters. However, before I could act, Mayza was already in the midst of things, kicking and pulling at one of the hunters. I decided to follow her lead, dropped my bag to the ground, and dived into the brawl.

Ghamen grunted as he flailed his limbs madly, trying to free himself. He finally broke loose, leaped for the bag and grabbed it, regaining his footing. I managed to push my opponent backwards and he tripped and fell onto a net filled with slippery fish that squirmed under him. I rushed over to Mayza and the two of us managed to knock the remaining hunter over. He landed on an empty net, and the two of us jumped onto him and tied him up. We looked up at each other, breathed a sigh of relief, and then . . . .

"Tommy! Look out!" she cried, grabbing my shoulders and pushing my face to the ground. I was taken from behind and yanked to my feet. The hunter I had knocked over was now holding me tight, but I thrashed fiercely, causing him to stagger. Ghamen tossed Mayza the bag and kicked my attacker in the back of the leg. He yelled out in pain and loosened his grip on me, just enough so that I could shake free. Angrily, the hunter turned to face Ghamen. At my feet I noticed a sack of seashells. I picked them up and twirled them over my head, sending them flying through the air. To my amazement they hit the hunter squarely in the back. The force was enough to send him crashing to the ground. He lay motionless for a few seconds and before he had time to recover, Ghamen and I were on him.

"Nice throw," Ghamen said with a smile. "I thought he was going to toss me overboard and then, WHACK, down he went." We wrapped up the last hunter, who was still slightly dazed, and tied the ends into a knot.

"Hurry up you two! This one is being difficult!" Mayza said, still sitting on the hunter that we had tied up earlier, whacking him with my bag. We made our way towards Mayza, who was near the entrance and still holding the bag. Her captive was in our way and unfortunately we were left with no other choice but to walk over him.

"Sorry, excuse me," I said, stepping on the hunter.

"Oops, excuse me," Ghamen said, following behind.

"See you later," Mayza said sarcastically, as she gave the hunter a tap on the head before jumping over him and leaving the boat.

"We'll get you! You can't hide from us!" the entangled hunter yelled out, as we ran from the boat and hurried into the city of Memphis.

10

Walk Like An Egyptian

The hustle and bustle of the morning was upon us as we entered the city's marketplace, shuffling quickly through the thick crowd. I tried to stay with Mayza and Ghamen, who were just up ahead, but they were moving too fast and I quickly fell behind.

"Excuse me . . . oops . . . pardon me . . . sorry . . . coming through!"

I was breathing hard and I wanted to call out to them, but it was hopeless. They were too far ahead and attracting attention to myself was the last thing I needed. All around me, the market got noisier and noisier. I was surrounded by a sea of people, who all seemed to be dressed the same way and doing the same things. It was overwhelming and I was starting to feel completely helpless as my two friends disappeared up ahead. I decided that I was now lost and as any good kids do when they're lost, I stopped dead in my tracks.

I stood still, looking all around me when suddenly someone grabbed my arm and pulled me from the busy street. "There you are. You really fell behind. Follow me," Mayza said, leading me behind a group of vendors at the side of the road. "It was a good thing we retraced our steps, Ghamen," Mayza said with relief, as we stopped for a rest.

"I thought I had lost you guys for good! I tried to keep up, but . . ."

"Tommy, it's okay. We were moving pretty fast. We actually should have kept a better eye on you, but then again, I don't think we could ever lose you!" Ghamen laughed, referring to my brown hair and colourful clothing.

"I know what you mean," I said, looking down at my clothes. "I must really stick out like a sore thumb."

"When did you hurt your thumb?"

"I didn't."

"Oh, but I thought you said . . ."

"No, I just stick out like . . . Ah, forget it."

"Okay," Ghamen said. "Oh! I have an idea. Follow me."

We headed down a side street and entered a small hut where we were met by a short little storekeeper. He greeted us and led me to a small stool where I sat down. I had no idea what was going on and before I could argue, the short little man was cutting my hair. Within minutes, Tommy T. Timson had his first Egyptian haircut.

"You look great, Tommy!" Mayza said, running her hands through my fresh cut. Ghamen laughed and patted me on the head, "Yes, that is much better. You will blend right in. HA-HA!"

"What about my clothes?"

"Here," Mayza said, handing me a white tunic that she had gotten from the storekeeper. "You can change your clothes over there."

There definitely was a new kid in town. The boy who had arrived in Egypt with blue jeans, a red coat and wavy brown hair was now wearing a white tunic, and the shortest black haircut you've ever seen. Yes, he even dyed my hair black!

I placed my old clothes into my bag and thanked the storekeeper. "Don't I at least get a lollipop?" I asked jokingly.

"A what?" Ghamen and Mayza replied together.

"Never mind," I said with a grin.

We headed back to the city's market area and began to walk among the townspeople. "So what are we going to do now?" I asked Ghamen, while looking around for Percival. I was so anxious to find him, and I had a sense that maybe he would be somewhere in town, just as he was the first time I'd met him.

"Where we are going is not far from here, however, it is not within walking distance so we are going to need to find someone who will take us there."

"How far is it?" I asked.

"I am not exactly sure, but if we find someone soon who is willing to help us, then it shouldn't take long at all."

Ghamen sounded confident that he had the situation under control, but I wasn't sure if travelling around Egypt was what I should be doing. I was eager to help my friends return the scrolls, but I needed to find Percival.

"I'm starving," Mayza declared, slapping me on the back. "Let's go get some food!"

"But we don't have any money," I said, as my stomach growled at the mention of food.

"Money?" asked Ghamen.

"What are you talking about?" Mayza asked, and I quickly realized that currency as I knew of it didn't exist, and that maybe I should just keep my mouth shut.

"How are we going to get the food?" I asked, trying to avoid the subject of money.

"We are going to have to trade something for it," explained Ghamen.

"What are we going to use? We don't have anything," Mayza said.

Ghamen stopped, turned around and smiled at his sister, "We're going to trade your hair."

"My hair? What are you talking about?" Mayza asked.

"We will have to cut your braid in order to trade it for food."

"No way, Ghamen! No way!" Mayza protested, crossing her arms in disappointment.

Ghamen took hold of his braid and added, "I will have to cut mine as well, or we won't be eating. Do you want us to steal food? You know what mom says."

"I know, she says that stealing hurts everyone," Mayza responded. Boy, I thought to myself, did she ever sound like my mom.

Mayza stood quietly and then took a look at my hair. "I guess we can't get any more hair from Tommy," she said teasingly, and then agreed to cut her braid. I quickly learned that people traded for goods they needed.

Within moments, some quick trades were made and the three of us, looking stranger than ever, sat down to eat. For lunch we had bread, vegetables, dried fish and fruit, including dates and figs. "Here Tommy, try this," Ghamen said, handing me something.

"What is it?" I asked, peeling the sticky morsel from his fingers.

"It is sweet. You will like it," he explained.

"Sweet? I love sweet things. In fact, where I come from, we have a sweet surprise day and my mom usually bakes me oatmeal cookies," I said, excited to try what he had given me.

"Go on then, try it," Ghamen insisted. I slowly raised it to my lips and took a small bite.

"Wow! This is really good!" I exclaimed excitedly, cramming the rest into my mouth.

"We know! We eat them all the time," Mayza said, as I wolfed the rest of it down.

"Maybe one day your mom will let us taste an oatmeal cookie, because I've never heard of such a thing," she said, gobbling down one of the tasty treats.

"Maybe one day," I said quietly, imaging the three of us sitting around my kitchen table.

"We better get moving," Ghamen said, as he stood up and wiped his face clean.

"Good idea," I said, looking around for Percival who had popped back into my mind. I still needed to find him, but for now I was just glad I wasn't eating his cooking! I don't think I could eat any of that black gross stuff again.

The sun was shining brightly and we started on our way through the marketplace to search for help. Walking through the streets was fascinating and a million questions about Egypt came to mind, but it was so crowded that I didn't have a chance to ask any of them, so I looked around and soaked in what I could. The first thing that I noticed was the number of animals. Men were walking through the town with oxen, donkeys and cows. Along the sides of the road, we saw farmers and tradesmen feeding livestock and tending to flocks of geese and ducks while children ran along the streets with pet dogs. There were animals everywhere, but to my relief, there were no hippos!

The smells of perfumes and spices mingled in the air. Merchants bartered their goods as they knelt under palm leaf shelters. Men with chisels were busy carving great stone blocks and artists were busy painting blocks that had already been carved, and the women all seemed to be sewing and working with fabrics.

We walked for some time, when out of the corner of my eye I saw someone covered in a long grey cloak. I left my friends and rushed across the street. I grabbed the man by the arm and turned him around. "Percival!" I shouted excitedly. The man turned, but to my dismay it wasn't him. My heart sank as the annoyed man took off down the street.

"Tommy! What are you doing?" Ghamen asked.

"Uh, nothing . . . I just thought . . ."

"Are you okay?" Mayza asked.

"Yes, I just thought I saw someone I knew."

"We had better keep going," Ghamen said.

We continued through the marketplace, when a small brown-haired animal crossed right over my feet. "AAAHHH! What is that?" I yelled, practically jumping into Ghamen's arms.

"It's a monkey," Mayza giggled, tempting the animal with a small fig she had kept from our meal. Slowly the monkey waddled its way to her, took the fig from her hand, and enjoyed the tasty snack. He hopped up onto her shoulder and began moving his arms, squealing softly.

"Hee-hee! You can pet him, Tommy. Many Egyptians keep monkeys for pets, but my mom says I'm still too young," Mayza said, while caressing the head of the jumpy little creature. I trusted Mayza and finally let go of Ghamen's arm. I reached up and patted the monkey's back. The hair was very soft and the monkey gave me a weird look.

"Why is he looking at me that way?" I asked.

"He likes you, Tommy," Mayza said, as the monkey quickly hopped from her shoulder to mine.

"Whoa! Get it off me!" I cried, staggering helplessly between Mayza and Ghamen.

"It's all right, Tommy," Mayza explained. "It won't hurt you. It just wants to be your friend."

"But it's eating my hair!"

"It's not eating your hair. It's just trying to hold onto you," Ghamen laughed.

"If you stop moving around like that, it won't have to hold your hair so tight," Mayza continued.

"Okay, okay," I said, slowing to a halt. The monkey loosened its grip and I finally had a chance to meet eye to eye with the furry little creature who sat atop my shoulder. "If we're going to be friends," I continued, "we can't eat each other's hair. Alright?" The monkey stared at me and then scurried off towards a merchant at the side of the street, who had attracted a group of people to his area by chanting to them.

Your darkest secrets and your biggest fears.
What will occur beyond your living years?

The crowd around him grew bigger and slowly we inched our way forward to take a closer look, but we couldn't see a thing, so we squeezed right to the front. The man continued to call out to the people, while the monkey rested on his shoulder. As we listened to the mysterious words, the monkey suddenly hopped from his shoulder and back onto mine. People pointed as he quickly climbed to the top of my head. I couldn't believe it! I had a monkey on my head! The crowd around us started to applaud as I stared bashfully at Mayza who was covering her mouth, trying not to laugh.

"I see that Yanny the monkey has chosen someone. I must have silence!" The man turned, his dark eyes burning into me, "Do you accept the challenge?"

Challenge? What challenge? A hush fell over the crowd and I looked at Mayza and Ghamen for support, but they were quiet too. The audience waited in anticipation. What was I supposed to say? I closed my eyes to think for a moment and then looked back at the man.

"I . . . accept."

11

Mummy Madness

I stared at the mysterious man, wondering what I had gotten myself into. The crowd around me whispered in excitement while I waited for the challenge. I reached up to pet Yanny, but to my surprise he was gone. He had found a safer place in the crowd, resting on another man's shoulder. This was definitely NOT monkey business.

Clear the way, the time is here.
Let him through, for death is near.

My jaw fell to the floor as another man standing eight feet tall, wearing a large black mask in the shape of a dog's head with pointy ears and a long blue mane, loomed in front of me. He wore a long white garment around his waist, and his muscular arms were covered in thick golden bracelets. He carried a gold painted chest, and everyone stood in silence while he walked towards me.

"Are you ready to face your *darkest secrets?*" asked the mysterious man.

I stood silent for a moment, and then replied, "Yes, I am."

"Are you ready to face your *biggest fears?*" he continued.

I gulped and replied, "Uh-huh."

"Do you know what will happen *beyond your living years?*" he finally asked. I tried to speak, but nothing came out. "**ANUBIS!**" he yelled aloud, motioning to the masked man. The masked man obeyed and lifted me up, placing me on a table that rested in the middle of the crowd. I lay still in fear as the mysterious man chanted.

> *Endless days, endless nights,*
> *Among the gods, eternally rest.*
> *Are you worthy? We shall see.*
> *It's time to take your ultimate test.*

He then looked at the crowd and continued.

> *Removing intestines, lungs and liver,*
> *Just the thought will make you quiver.*

I lifted my head, and looked at him as if he were crazy. The crowd laughed but I didn't think it was funny at all.

> *Brains, brains, everyone knows,*
> *With a hook and through the nose.*

Brains through the nose? WHAT? I had to get out of here! I tried to roll off the table, but the masked man stopped me. The audience laughed as I rolled from side to side, trying like mad to get away. I couldn't believe what was happening!

"This man is CRAZY!" I yelled. "I like my brains exactly where they are, thank you very much!"

"My little friend, I also like your brains where they are. We are street performers and as you can see, you have made our show a hit!" he smiled, turning back to the people who applauded loudly.

The show continued and the two performers talked about the art of **mummification**. I learned that the masked man was playing Anubis, the jackal-headed god of **embalming**. He was the protector of the dead and was always involved in the embalming process–a process that transforms bodies into mummies. I learned that the heart and lungs and all the other internal organs were removed, but fortunately, the person was already dead–or maybe that's unfortunate. Anyway, the organs were often placed in special containers for preservation and buried alongside the body. The brains were also removed, and to my disgusted surprise, they did indeed pull them out through the nose. GROSS!

The man posing as Anubis continued, "The body of the dead person is stuffed and covered with salt which helps break up different fats. Close to forty days later, when the body is completely dried, it is anointed with perfumes and spices," he said, as he held up an opened bottle and passed it through the crowd filling the air with a sweet aroma. The man then held up a small golden bracelet. "Jewellery is then placed all around the body, which is finally wrapped to form the mummy. Magical amulets are often placed within the wrappings and the head of the mummy is sometimes covered with a mask. When the preparation is complete, the body is placed inside the **sarcophagus**." He then held up some cloth and gave me a friendly grin, "Would you like to be a mummy for a day, my young friend?"

I raised my eyebrows, looked at Mayza and Ghamen and decided to go for it. I figured I had nothing to lose, as long as my insides were staying on the inside!

The two men crossed my arms over my chest and began to wrap me in long strips of linen. The crowd watched as the two men wrapped each limb separately, including my fingers and toes. They mentioned that an actual body might be covered in up to twenty layers of cloth! Slowly and carefully, the men wrapped my body from head to toe, finishing with my face. The audience applauded with delight as I lay on the table in my body cast, completely mummified, when . . . .

"Tommy, Tommy! They're back!" It was Ghamen and he was standing right beside the table, tearing at my wrappings.

"Who's back? What are you talking about?" I mumbled, through a small opening at my mouth. My eyes and ears were completely covered, but I could hear him faintly through the cloth.

"They found us!" Ghamen yelled into my ear. Fear was hanging on his every word. I tensed up and turned my head towards his voice, but I couldn't see a thing.

"The hunters?" I asked.

"NO! THE THIEVES! They're coming this way! They've found us!"

"WHAT? Are you serious? We have to get out of here!" I struggled to get up off the table but I couldn't move.

"Tommy, you're in no shape to go anywhere right now," Ghamen said, trying to free me from the cloth. "They've already spotted us! Mayza and I have to leave. The bag is under the table. It will be safe there. STAY HERE! You are well hidden. We will come back for you later."

"Wait . . . ." I tried to speak but it was too late. They were gone and I was alone.

I tried to lie on the table as Ghamen had ordered but I couldn't do it. We were all in trouble and I had to do something to help my friends. I squirmed around and slowly the cloth began to loosen from around my body. I was able to free an arm and I reached blindly under the table and found my bag. My legs were still wrapped tight, but I kept squirming until I was able to stand up.

Anubis continued, "So, as you can see my friends, our mummy is now complete. He is lying . . . WAS lying over there! Where are you going? The show has not ended!"

"Well, it's time I wrapped it up! I have to get out of here, NOW!" I said firmly, bouncing my way past the performers and into the crowd.

I picked up a good pace, moving through the crowd and down the street. I didn't know where I was going but I was moving smoothly, when . . . UGH! I tripped and fell to the ground. I tried to stand up but I couldn't bend my knees. I rolled around in the dirt trying to get up, when I felt a hand grab the cloth from my forehead. RRRRIP! The linen loosened around my eyes and I could finally see again!

I stared up at an elderly merchant who was selling tools at the side of the road. Talk about landing in the right place at the right time! He helped loosen the linen around my body and after a few seconds, I could move freely again. I yanked at the wrappings around my face and threw them to the ground. "Thank you!" I said, and then hustled away.

With cloth dangling from my body, I scurried through the busy streets in search of my friends but found that everyone looked the same and I didn't know which way to go. I was running in circles, and Mayza and Ghamen were nowhere to be found.

I headed down a side street and found a small alleyway. I followed it into a dead end, removed my bag and sat down against a wall.

"I should have stayed where I was!" I yelled aloud. "Now they'll never find me!" I was furious, and grabbed my bag tight, lifting it up. I stared at it, and out of frustration threw it against the wall in front of me. It hit the ground with a thud, and my textbook fell out onto the dusty road. I sat against the stone wall, feeling completely lost and scared. What was I going to do? This couldn't be happening to me. I began to tremble with fear. I drew my legs close to my body, sank my face into my knees and began to cry.

12

Purr-fect Timing

I sat against the wall feeling scared and lost. I didn't know what else to do. I was exhausted and fed up with everything. I was fed up with time travel, I was fed up with running from bandits and knights and feeling scared and alone, and I was really upset that Percival had abandoned me in this desert. I wasn't having any fun and I just wanted to go home. Why was this happening to me? I kicked the dirt and sent a cloud of dust and pebbles flying through the alley. How was I going to get home? I didn't know where I was. I had lost my friends and without Percival I would have no way of finding the door, let alone opening it. I began thinking of home again—of my parents and Tina and all my friends. I would have given anything to be home with them. I would have given anything to see my family and friends.

I wiped the tears from my eyes and looked around the alley. It was plain and empty except for my bag and the mess I had made when I had thrown it against the wall. One of my textbooks was spread across the ground and one of my notebooks was lying not too far from my foot. It was the same notebook that I used to write letters to my pen pal. I reached with my foot and dragged it towards me. I picked it up and opened it to my last letter. I remembered writing it. I was in a bedroom of King John's castle. The air was stale and I was sitting on a lumpy bed, but I was excited and felt happy. I glanced over the long letter. It talked of Sir William and the joust between Sir Henry and the king and the banquet. I still couldn't believe how much food there had been! The pen I had used was still in the notebook, so I picked it up and instinctively started to write another letter.

I started the letter by asking Anna how she was doing and what she had been up to. I told her about the magical door and about the thieves, the hunters and my friends and then I smiled and started to think about how nuts it all sounded. There was no way she was going to believe any of it, but I kept writing because it calmed me down and made me feel better. As always, I finished the letter by signing at the bottom: Your pen pal, Tommy T. Timson.

I looked over the letter to make sure I hadn't spelled anything wrong and smiled, thinking about how crazy this whole adventure was. I could barely believe it myself and I was living it! I then remembered the girl whom Percival had told me of and who was also travelling through time. I guess she would be the only person who would really believe me. I began to think of her and wondered if she was going through the same things that I was. Maybe she was. Maybe she wasn't. Maybe she was having a great time on her journey. I mean, I couldn't imagine her having a worse time than I was having.

I closed my notebook, took a deep breath and looked up at the sky. I tried to imagine what my parents and Tina were doing. I hoped they weren't too worried. I had only been gone a little more than a day, but I knew that my mother would be worried out of her mind and that made me feel even worse. I knew that I had to try my best to get home. I couldn't give up now, especially since I had come so far. I remembered my dad, who used to tell me that the only way to succeed in life is to try your best at everything you do. That's what I needed to do. I needed to try my best to get out of here. I had to put all my fears aside and get out of this alleyway and find my friends.

I rubbed my eyes and stood up. I was feeling tired but I knew I had to keep moving. I picked up my bag and put my notebook inside. I then walked over to my textbook and bent down to pick it up. I noticed that it was my history textbook and that it was opened to the Medieval Times! Wow! I sat down and put my bag aside. I picked up the book and started reading it, searching excitely for my name. They had to have mentioned me! I saved the king! I read through it and found the Magna Carta, and then I found a painting of King John, which I felt didn't capture his likeness at all. I searched and searched but couldn't find my name anywhere. As if! They could have at least said something about me.

Then a light bulb went off in my head. Well a light bulb didn't really go off in my head, but I thought of a really good idea. I turned to the index of the book and looked for the Egyptian section. A, B, C, D, E, F, E . . .

E . . . Egypt. I found it and turned to the page. There were pictures of pyramids and of cities and even a map. A map! All right! Maybe I could use this map to help me navigate through Egypt.

On page 315, there was a picture of three large pyramids. One of the pyramids stood taller than the other two. They looked familiar and then I remembered that I had seen these pyramids when I landed here! I began to read.

> The pyramids at Giza rest peacefully in the morning sun. These great structures have stood for thousands of years and are a beautiful display of the Ancient Egyptian culture. The largest of the three pyramids is known as The **Great Pyramid**, built by Fourth Dynasty King Khufu. No other pyramid in the history of Egypt has stood as tall. Along with the Great Pyramid sit two others. Khufu's son, King Khephren, built his pyramid beside his father's, hoping to continue in his father's greatness. King Menkaura's pyramid, the smallest of the three, also rests near King Khufu's masterpiece.

I continued to read. Then suddenly, the pyramids began to sway back and forth on the page, which really freaked me out. I dropped the book to the ground and slid back, but I couldn't take my eyes off the page. The words around the picture disappeared, and the pyramids faded away leaving the page blank.

A new picture formed on the page. This time it was a bird's eye view of a city. I picked the book back up and stared deeply at the scene. I could see rows and rows of houses built close together and streets filled with people. I looked closer at the picture and realized that the people were moving!

I leaned over the book and watched the image zoom in on the city until it eventually came upon an individual who sat all alone. I lifted the book up to my eyes to get a better view, and when I did, I noticed that the person in the page was holding a book in the same way that I was! Something was weird here. I lifted a hand off the book, as did the person in the picture. Wow! It was me!

"What's going on here?" I said to myself, when suddenly the image changed to a picture of a single pyramid, which rested atop a sandy hill. There were four symbols carved in the stone above the entrance. I ran a finger over the bizarre shapes and as I did, a spark of light suddenly exploded on the page, causing me to shut my eyes. When I opened them, the picture of the pyramids at Giza had returned, and my textbook was back to teaching history.

I quickly flipped through the Egypt section of the book, reading it for anything else that could help me out, when all of a sudden I heard a scratching sound behind my back. Startled, I slammed the book shut and turned my head to see what it was. I saw something small dash around the corner and out of sight but it moved so quickly that I wasn't able to get a good look at it. My heart was racing and I stood up just in case I would have to make a run for it. I held my breath, trying not to make any noise, but it didn't return. My heart slowed and I shrugged it off as nothing and sat back down to go over the Egypt section once more before I tried to find my friends.

I opened the book and found my spot when I heard the scratching sound again. I jumped to my feet and found myself staring into the eyes of a dark grey cat. "It's just a cat," I sighed with relief. We looked at each other curiously and for some reason the cat seemed very familiar to me, as if I had come across it before. I felt like it wanted something, so I approached and it meowed. "What is it, kitty?" I asked, trying to sooth it with a soft, comforting voice. "Are you hungry?" I realized that even if the cat answered, I had no food to give it so I changed the subject. "Are you lost?"

The cat meowed again and began to move towards me. I knelt down and stretched my hand out to greet it. The cat rubbed its face against my hand and started to purr. That's when I noticed it was carrying something with its tail. I couldn't believe it! The cat was carrying my watch! "This is amazing! Where did you find this? I'd hug you but I'm allergic to cats so I can't really touch you but WOW!"

I was super excited to have it back and fumbled with it, trying to get it on my wrist. I put it on but was scared to look at it. I could only hope that it hadn't yet reached *a quarter past three.* I held my breath in anticipation and looked down at it but there was too much dust covering it to tell what time it was. I wiped off the dust and WHEW, it was 1:10 pm. Yes! I had just over two hours to figure out how I was going to find the key and the door. I was really happy to have my watch back and knew I had a chance to get through this.

I looked out through the alley and decided that it was time to go. I didn't know which direction to take but I knew that I had to move on while I still had time. I stood up, collected my things, and heaved my bag onto my back. Then I said good-bye to the cat and left to find my friends.

13

Relief Beyond Belief

It was early afternoon and the sun beat down, high overhead. I stepped from the alleyway and the dark grey cat let out a slow whine, "Meoww."

I stopped and turned around to find the cat staring up at me. "What's wrong, kitty?" I asked. "I have to go and find my friends." It let out another slow whine and ran quickly past me, out to the corner of the street. It turned back to look at me and then meowed again. "What is it? Where are you going?" I wasn't sure what to do, so I walked up to it, but it dashed off and stopped a short distance away. It turned its head again and meowed. "What are you doing?" I asked. What was it doing? What was I doing? I was talking to this cat as if it was a human being. Maybe the heat was getting to me but I still felt there was something very familiar about this cat that I couldn't put my finger on. The cat meowed again and I decided that it wanted me to follow it, so I did.

The cat dashed off down the street so I stepped up my pace and followed it as fast as I could. I learned that following a cat isn't the easiest thing in the world to do, even if it wants to be followed. The cat scurried through the crowds, crawling under fruit stands and over vending carts. I kept my eye on it, losing it for only seconds at a time. It was tricky and I kept bumping into things but I eventually got the hang of it. I hopped over boxes and slithered around people until finally the cat stopped in front of a small tent and turned to look back at me.

"Is this it? Is this where you wanted to take me?" I asked, looking around finding nothing more than a few ratty old tents and some garbage scattered along the streets. "So what now?" I asked the cat, as I walked over and crouched down to touch it. "What now?" I repeated to myself, looking around for anything that would give me an idea of what to do next. Just then a hand grabbed me around the mouth and hauled me into a tent.

"MMPPHH!"

There was no light inside the tent and I was forced into a chair. I felt as though I was about to breathe my last breath, when a light flickered from a lamp that lit the inside of the tent.

"Tommy, it's okay. It's us, Mayza and Ghamen." I was so scared that I wasn't responding, so Mayza and Ghamen had to shake me from side to side.

"Tommy, it's all right. You are safe," Ghamen said, trying to comfort me.

I shook my head and said, "If you EVER scare me like that again, I'll . . . I'll . . ."

"Ha! You're funny, Tommy," replied Ghamen.

"You should have seen the look on your face. You were so scared, I was sure you were going to wet your pants," Mayza said, trying not to laugh.

"Thanks a lot. Like I really needed that. I've been through a lot today, you know."

"We know. We're sorry, but Mayza saw you and we had to get you in here as fast as we could. This place is crawling with scum."

"Yeah, and the thieves are still around here somewhere. We're really sorry, Tommy. We just needed to get you out of sight," Mayza added.

"It's okay. It's all right. I'm just glad to see you guys," I said, standing up to give them both a hug.

"Where did you end up? We went back for you after losing the thieves, but you were nowhere to be found."

"I know, I'm sorry. I got caught up with everything and I was really worried about you two and I went after you but then I got lost and . . ."

"It's all right, Tommy. The important thing is that we are all together again," reassured Ghamen.

"Have a seat. I will get you something to drink," said Mayza, as she walked over to a small cupboard and brought out some cups. Ghamen and I sat down at a table that had been placed against the wall of the small tent. The tent was a mess and had obviously been deserted for some time. Mayza poured us each a drink and brought them to the table. She gave us each a cup and then sat down on the remaining stool.

"Thank you," I said, quickly chugging it down. "This is good. What is it?"

"It's a mixture of fruits and herbs. It's a popular drink on hot days like today," explained Mayza.

91

"We picked it up in the market when we were looking for you. Rest and enjoy your drink," said Ghamen.

I took another sip and felt better. It was cooler in the tent and I was glad that I had found my friends again. I noticed that my watch was in plain view and I quickly put my arm out of sight, under the table. "Where exactly are we?" I asked.

"We are not sure ourselves. We found this tent and it was empty, so we decided to stay here for a while. There are some bad people in this part of town and we have to be careful not to be seen," explained Ghamen.

"And even though we lost track of the thieves, we are afraid that they are still looking for us," added Mayza.

"We were about to go back out and search for you, when Mayza spotted you through the slit in the entrance of the tent."

"Yes, that was very lucky. How on earth did you know where to find us?" Mayza asked.

"I didn't know where to find you. I just followed a cat and he brought me here."

"A cat?" Ghamen questioned.

"Yes, I was in an alley and then this cat showed up with my watch and then . . ."

"Your what?" asked Ghamen, who was very puzzled.

"My watch . . . Uh . . . I mean this cat was watching me. Yeah, it was watching me and I thought it was weird that it was watching me. I mean it was really watching me, you know?"

"Yes, yes, it was watching you. We get it. Now go on," said Mayza, quickly becoming impatient.

I took a deep breath and resumed my story, "So I followed the cat and he brought me here."

"That's incredible! Actually, many Egyptians believe that some cats are sacred. Some have even been mummified! Now I can see why," Ghamen grinned, as he got up to refresh our drinks.

I sneaked a peek at my watch. It was getting late and I knew that time would quickly run out on me if I didn't do something soon. I needed to find Percival, but in order to do that I would have to leave the tent to look for him and I knew the thieves were still looking for us. I couldn't believe that he would just forget about me like that and leave me stranded here. I thought that he was trustworthy and now he had let me down and I knew I couldn't make this journey on my own. I didn't know where I was or where to go, or whom to see or anything. If I hadn't had friends like Mayza and Ghamen, I'd probably still be lost in the desert somewhere.

I looked at the two of them as they rested and sipped their drinks. They were good friends and I was lucky to have found them. I thought more carefully about Mayza and Ghamen and started to wonder whether they could help me. I knew I was supposed to keep all of this a secret but what good would that do if I could never see my family again, and besides, Percival had abandoned me. I decided that it was time to take matters into my own hands and forget about that stupid wizard.

My heart raced as I went over all the ways that I could tell my friends about my journey without looking like a complete wacko. Should I tell them about my home? Should I tell them about the magical door or the key? My thoughts were racing a mile a minute until I couldn't take it anymore and then I finally stood up and shoved out my arm saying, "This is a watch! This is what the cat brought back to me. A watch! See?"

"Are you all right, Tommy?" asked Ghamen, standing up out of concern.

"I don't know. I need you guys to listen to me. I'm in trouble and I don't have much time."

"Take a deep breath. You're going to be all right," said Ghamen.

"Okay, but I need you guys to listen carefully. What I'm about to tell you is going to sound crazy and you probably won't believe me, but I'm going to tell you anyway," I said, as I motioned for Ghamen to sit down.

"Are you going to tell us you're from the future?" Mayza said, as she turned to Ghamen and chuckled.

"Ha . . . that's funny . . . now where to begin?" I replied nervously.

"Just spit it out. We're your friends. Of course we'll believe you, unless you tell us you're from the future. Then we'll just think you're crazy," Ghamen said, as they both laughed. "I'm kidding," he continued. "Go on, tell us."

"Okay, here it goes. I'm from the future."

"I knew it! I knew you were from the future!" Mayza said. "I told you he was from the future. Nobody has shoes like his! Look at those things," she said to Ghamen.

"Keep going, Tommy," said Ghamen.

I could feel the pressure lift and couldn't wait to continue telling them, so I took another deep breath and let it pour out, "I'm lost in time and I met this wizard and he's supposed to help me but I can't find him and there are these doors that I have to find and I never know where I'll end up and when I get there my clothes never match anyone else's and I stand out and people stare at me and I have these letters that I write and I have this watch that I have to hide and I never know who to trust and it's really hot in here. Are you guys hot?"

"Tommy, Tommy, slow down, it's all right, we believe you," said Ghamen sympathetically, placing his hand on my shoulder. "It's going to be all right," he continued, "just tell us what you need us to do."

I took a deep breath and a sip of my drink. "So you believe me?" I asked hesitantly.

"We're friends, aren't we?" Mayza said smiling.

I felt as though a thousand pound weight had been lifted from my shoulders. It had been really good to share all that with them. It made me feel a lot better. "Okay, this is my problem. In a short time from now, a magical door is going to appear somewhere and I need to find it. The problem is I don't know where it's going to appear."

"How can we find out?" asked Mayza.

"That's the thing. The wizard is supposed to tell me where, but he's not here. He's also supposed to give me a big key to open the door so that . . ."

"Did you say key?" asked Ghamen.

"Yeah, a big key. He's supposed to give me a big key so I can . . ." Mayza and Ghamen's eyes bulged out as they looked at each other in amazement.

"What's wrong?" I asked.

"Does it look like this?" she asked, pulling out a large key that hung on a string around her neck. I looked at it carefully and reached out to touch it. As my fingers touched the key, a wave of energy surged through my body and knocked me off my stool. I looked up at it from where I lay on the ground. There it was, the magical key, hanging around her neck. I smiled, knowing that I had finally found the key.

14

A Key For Me

I looked closely at the key that hung around Mayza's neck. It was very different from the one I had received from Percival. It was much bigger and it was made of gold, with strange symbols carved along its shaft. Mayza held it between her fingers, and smiled as I stared in wonder at it.

I scratched my head and asked, "Where on earth did you find this?"

Mayza's eyes filled with tears and Ghamen placed an arm around her shoulder. The light of the lamp glowed against her face as she wiped a tear from her cheek. She looked at the key lovingly and then held it to her heart.

"My father gave me this key," she said sadly, rubbing her eyes. She straightened up and cleared her throat, "Tommy, this key is a gift from my father and it will always be a memory of his life." She ran her fingers along the length of the key and continued, "When he gave me this key a few years ago, he also gave me this." She reached into her robe and took out a piece of folded papyrus. She smiled shyly, unfolded the paper and began to read.

My dearest Mayza,

I have had this special key for some time now and today, I am passing it onto you. This is a key that represents strength and courage. One day while walking along the banks of the Nile, a crocodile attacked me. With a vicious swipe of its tail, I found myself lying on my back, at its mercy. I turned my head and saw this key lying in the mud. I grabbed it and lifted it up towards the mouth of the crocodile. Bewildered, I stared at the key as it sparkled bright green and then watched the animal slam its jaws shut, fleeing back to the water.

To this day, I still do not comprehend what happened, nor has the key sparkled since, but I do believe that it saved my life and brought me back home to my family. May this key always be a token of the love we share.

Papa

Mayza removed the key from her neck and looked at me, "I have always kept this close to my heart, and while I will never forget its meaning, I know now that this key belongs to you. You must take it and find the magical door." She reached out, and placed the key in my hand.

Ghamen pointed at the key and started yelling excitedly, "Look! Look at the key, Mayza!" The strange symbols on the key were glowing bright green and none of us could believe it. This was definitely the magical key, but one question still remained unanswered. Where on earth was the door?

15

Secret Of The Symbols

It was 1:40 pm and we sat quietly around the table finishing our drinks. We had been through a lot in the last little while and it was nice to finally have a rest. I closed my eyes and took a deep breath, knowing that we still had a lot to do. I had to help my friends save their mother and then make my way to the magical door, wherever that was.

I leaned over to place the key in my bag when I remembered something. "Wait a minute!" I yelled, pointing at the four symbols. "I've seen these markings before! I saw them in my history book!" I reached for my knapsack, grabbed the book and opened it up to explain what had happened in the alleyway.

"What do you think the markings mean, Tommy?" Mayza asked.

"I don't know what they mean but I remember seeing them in my book. Four symbols just like these were carved above the entrance of a pyramid!" I explained, running my fingers along the carvings.

Ghamen clapped his hands, his eyes sparkling with excitement in the light of the lamp. "I've got it! When I was young, my father told me a story about an old pyramid which lies on the edge of Memphis. It was built mysteriously by an ancient tribe and above the entrance are carved four symbols that represent the greatest riddle of all time. Inside the pyramid, a maze was built that was so intricate that all who entered were lost and never seen again. Deep within this maze, the tribe placed the tomb of their leader. The story says that the meaning of the four symbols can be found inside this tomb, revealing the great riddle. It is said that whoever can unlock the mystery of the riddle will be awarded the most beautiful treasure ever known. I think your book was trying to tell you that your door will be inside this pyramid, and I think this key will give us some answers. Let me see it again."

I watched while he examined it in the light, carefully studying the symbols. I envisioned myself walking through the maze in search of the hidden tomb and my imagination ran wild, thinking about what I would find inside.

"Hold the key, Tommy," Ghamen said, handing it to me. I placed the key in the palm of my hand and the symbols began to glow again. "Now, turn it over." I followed Ghamen's instructions and slowly turned the key over. To our surprise there was an inscription that had not been there before. "I knew it! There is more! Look here!" said Ghamen, eagerly waiting for me to read it.

"This is great, Ghamen, but I can't read it! It's written in weird letters and pictures," I said.

"It's Egyptian writing, Tommy! It's called **hieroglyphics**. Let me see that." I moved the key towards Ghamen and he began to read.

You who hold me, hold so much,
You now have the magic touch.
Put the symbols to the test,
Fit me in the place that's best.
Always stand, brave and strong,
Only aim for right, not wrong.
Start this path, but please take care,
It's no game of truth or dare.

"That's all I can understand," Ghamen said. "The inscription continues, but in another language I've never seen before." I looked carefully at the key, and nearly fell over. The inscription was very small but I could see the words clearly and smiled because they were written in English!

"You guys won't believe this! It's written in my language! It's written in English!" I began to read aloud.

You'll be lost without a clue,
Wondering what on earth to do.
Enter into dark and grey,
Twists and turns won't seem like play.
So listen carefully, my good friend,
Make good choices to the end.
Solve the riddle or you'll see,
You'll be stuck here holding me.

"I'm never getting home! This key is telling me that I have to solve the riddle before I can open the door! That means I have to find the hidden tomb, and even if I find it, I still don't know what the symbols are trying to tell me. This is terrible." I dropped my head and stared at the floor.

"Neither do we, Tommy, but we are here to help you," Mayza said. "We can do it. You must believe and you must trust."

"And, we already have a head start. I know where the pyramid is!" Ghamen said, putting an arm on my shoulder.

They were right. I still had a long way to go but I had to stay confident, and besides, I had two great friends by my side. I leaned over, placed the key in my bag and zipped it up. "First, we must save your mother. Let's get out of here and return those scrolls," I said, standing up from the table.

"That sounds like a plan to me," said Ghamen, when the flaps of our tent were torn apart flooding the room with sunlight that blinded us all.

"Well, look who we have here," a deep voice said from the entrance of our shelter. "Just the people we've been looking for. HA! HA! HA!"

16

Stumble In The Road

The sun poured in, blinding the three of us as we turned our heads and shielded our eyes with our hands. I peered between my fingers and saw two large silhouettes standing in front of us. Their voices were upsettingly familiar but the sun was preventing me from recognizing who they were.

"We have been tracking you all day," said the deep voice stepping forward.

The three of us stood frozen in the shadows of whoever had come for us. The two shapes approached, letting go of the tent flaps, causing them to fall back, shutting out the sun.

"I believe you have something that belongs to us," the voice said.

I lowered my hand from my face and in horror realized that the thieves had found us! I glanced over at Ghamen and Mayza who were both shaking in fear.

"Aren't you happy to see us? Surely you didn't think you could get away from us that easily?" said the leader, walking around carelessly exploring the contents of the messy room. "So where are they?" he continued, taking a swig of juice from the jug that we had left on the counter.

"Where are what?" I asked, breaking our silence.

The thief spit out the juice in disgust and walked over to me. He grabbed me by the ear and said, "Don't get smart with me. You know what we're after! Now where are they?"

I knew that he was talking about the scrolls, but I also knew that he hadn't seen Ghamen swipe them from the campsite. I thought that if I was able to convince him that we didn't know what they were talking about, maybe they would leave us alone.

"Really, I don't know what you're talking about," I said, trembling in my shoes. The thief released my ear and stepped toward Ghamen.

"How about you?" said the leader, grabbing hold of Ghamen's ear, nearly lifting him off the ground. Ghamen stared stubbornly into the eyes of the thief and said nothing. The frustrated thief released Ghamen's ear and turned to face his companion. "Looks as though nobody wants to talk to me," he said, rubbing his chin. "If they're not going to say anything, then they won't need their tongues!" he shouted angrily, reaching into his cloak and revealing a long sharp dagger.

Our eyes nearly popped out of their sockets at the thought of losing our tongues, and to prove to the thief that I did indeed require mine, I yelled as loud as I could, "RUUNNN!" The three of us dashed to the back corner of the tent where there was a break in the material, but just as we pulled the flap aside, we came face to face with the other thieves who had been waiting outside. They grabbed hold of us and carried us back inside the tent.

We were dragged to the table where they shoved us into the chairs, keeping their filthy hands secure on our shoulders. The thief with the dagger approached us. "We'll start with this one," he said, pointing his blade at me.

I couldn't believe what was happening to me. These guys were nuts! They were out of control! I had to do something or say something, anything to get out of this. Then something that my mom had always said popped into my head and spilled out of my mouth, "I think you need to manage your anger in a more constructive way."

"What did you say?" yelled the dagger wielding thief.

"Uh, I don't know," I said, which was partially true.

"Hey," interrupted one of the other thieves. "Look what I found," he said, holding up my knapsack.

"Give me that!" ordered the leader, who, to my delight, was quickly losing interest in the removal of my tongue. He snatched the bag from his partner and fought with the zipper, which he had problems with, probably because he had never come across one before. He gave up in a huff and threw it in my lap. "Open this!" he yelled. I looked at Mayza and Ghamen who were sitting quietly across from me and slowly unzipped the bag. The thief took the bag from me and rummaged through it, finding the scrolls. "Ah-ha! What do we have here?" he said, taking a scroll from the bag and unravelling it. "Perfect!" he continued, stepping away from the table, completely engrossed in the scroll. "Now we can continue our journey.

With the help of these scrolls, we will become the richest men in the land!" he boasted.

"Those don't belong to you!" Ghamen snapped. The thief who was holding his shoulder, pressed him further back into his seat. "Those belong to the **Pharaoh**!" he continued.

"They used to belong to the Pharaoh. Now they belong to me!" the leader barked, rolling up the scroll.

"You traitor!" yelled Mayza. "You betrayed our parents!" she shouted angrily.

"Quiet!" yelled the thief, as he held up the scroll. "You have cost us valuable time and I will not stand here and listen to you whine!" he said, placing the scroll back in my bag.

"Please," I begged, "give us back the scrolls. We need to return them to free their mother."

"Mother?" snapped the leader. "HA! It is too late for her. This afternoon she will be sentenced to join your father!"

"You're a liar!" yelled Mayza.

"I am a thief, not a liar," he stated with a grin. "Now get rid of these three before they cause us anymore trouble," he barked at his companions, who were still holding us firmly in our seats.

They picked us up and carried each of us under their arms, as if they had done this many times before. "What do you want us to do with them?" one of the thieves asked.

"Anything! Just get rid of them. I don't ever want to see them again!" their leader said, as he returned his dagger to its sheath. "I am going for supplies. I will be at the shop on the corner. After you have disposed of them, I want you to meet me there," he instructed, as he tucked my bag under his arm and darted out of the tent.

We left the tent and were carried down the deserted streets of the decaying neighbourhood. The thieves were walking beside each other which allowed Mayza, Ghamen and I to see each other clearly. I thought of yelling for help, but there was no one around who could offer any. The thieves were involved in a heavy debate over what to do with us, which gave us an opportunity to discuss our next move.

"What do we do now?" I asked Ghamen.

"I don't know. Any ideas, Mayza?" Ghamen responded.

"I'm stuck. He's holding me really tight. I can hardly breathe," gasped Mayza, struggling to free herself.

"We could bite their hands," I suggested.

"Bite them? I'm not biting them. Look at this hand. It's disgusting!" Mayza replied.

"Ghamen," I continued, "bite his hand."

"I'm not biting his hand. You bite his hand."

"His hands are filthy," I said.

"Exactly!" responded Ghamen.

"Well, what are we going to do?" I asked the two of them.

"I have a plan. Just follow my lead," Ghamen said quietly, as the thieves stopped at the back entrance of a shop.

"This will do," said the thief who was carrying me. They brought us into a large, empty shop that looked like it had been deserted for years. A thick layer of white dust covered every inch of space and as we moved through the room, the dust on the floor flew up into our faces causing us to cough. Within seconds we all looked like we had been covered in flour.

"What a mess," groaned one of the thieves, swatting at the dust around his face. I looked around the room and all I could see were rows on rows of sarcophagi. They were all lined up against each other, and the sight of them under the layer of dust gave me the creeps.

"We'll put them in these. They won't be able to get out," one of the thieves suggested to the other two.

"What?" I yelled. "You can't put us in those!"

"Are those your last words?" said the thief who was carrying me. He unlatched a sarcophagus and opened it up. The other two thieves followed his lead, opening two more. Dust flew everywhere as they disturbed the stillness in the shop. "No!" we each screamed, as we were thrown in one by one, the doors slamming shut behind us.

"By the time anyone finds you, you'll be nothing but a worthless pile of rotten flesh," said the thief who had been carrying me.

The three of us began to yell and scream but it was no use. The thieves had left us to rot inside the old Egyptian coffins.

17

Lucky 'Break'

I pushed the light on my watch and saw that it was 2:00 pm. I had just over an hour to get my bag back, save their mother and find the pyramid that hopefully would lead me to the magical door, but first I had to find a way out of this sarcophagus.

"Are you two all right?" asked Ghamen, from inside his box.

"No! I'm not all right! I'm locked inside a sarcophagus!" yelled Mayza.

"I thought you had a plan," I said to Ghamen.

"I did. It just didn't work."

"I can see that!" yelled Mayza.

"What was it anyway?" I asked out of curiosity.

"At some point we were supposed to run," Ghamen explained.

"We didn't run," I said, thinking it over.

"No, we didn't," Ghamen replied.

"Can either of you get out?" Mayza asked. Ghamen and I pushed with all our strength on the lids of our coffins, but they wouldn't budge.

"How are we supposed to get out of these things?" I yelled.

"We're not supposed to! There's a latch that secures the lid, but it's on the outside," Ghamen explained.

"I hate the dark!" yelled Mayza, as I pushed the light button on my watch, which lit up the inside of the sarcophagus just enough so I could see around.

"I have a light. Maybe there's a latch on the inside?" I said.

"Where did you get the light from?" asked Ghamen.

"It's built into my watch," I answered, looking closely for a way out.

"I hate the dark!" Mayza yelled again, kicking the inside of her sarcophagus.

"Do you see anything?" Ghamen asked me.

"I don't know. I can't see anything yet. Maybe it's on the other side," I said, turning around to run my hands along the back of the box.

"Do you see anything now?" Ghamen asked.

"No. There's nothing. We're going to have to come up with something . . ." Before I could finish my sentence, the lid of my sarcophagus opened.

"I hate the dark, Tommy," Mayza said calmly with a smile.

"Mayza! How did you get out?" I asked in amazement.

"These things are really old. All you have to do is kick them and they break right open," she explained, helping me out.

"What's going on out there?" Ghamen shouted anxiously.

"It's all right, hold on," I said, fumbling with his latch. We opened the lid and Ghamen stepped out, looking confused.

"How did you get out?" Ghamen asked.

"Mayza just kicked it open," I explained.

"Yeah, it was easy. Now let's get out of here and find those thieves," she said confidently.

"They said they were going to get supplies. Do either of you know where they can do that?" I asked.

"I don't," replied Ghamen.

"Me neither," responded Mayza.

"I guess we'll have to find it on our own. We had better get a move on. If what they said is true about your mother, then we have no time to waste." The three of us turned to leave when we heard a scream come from the other side of the room.

"What was that?" asked Mayza quietly.

"Look! There's a man standing over there in the corner. He is holding a broom," explained Ghamen. The three of us watched as the man continued to scream in horror.

"What's wrong with him?" I asked.

"I don't know. He's just standing there screaming," Mayza said.

"He looks like he's seen a mummy," added Ghamen, our eyes slowly turning towards three open coffins and then down to our white bodies.

"He doesn't think we're mummies, does he?" I asked with a smirk. The three of us walked over to him but he was becoming more hysterical with each step we took. We called out reassuringly that we were not mummies and that in fact we were alive and well and carried all our organs within us, but he was so upset, he couldn't understand a word we were saying. When we reached him, he crouched down in the corner and held the broom up over his head to protect himself. He looked so scared and I was starting to feel really bad for him. I tried my best to wipe the dust from my body, but it wasn't coming off, so I tried to talk to him calmly, because if I could get him to relax, then I could also get directions to the supply shop.

"Stay back! I am sorry for disturbing your rest. Please don't hurt me," said the man, frightened out of his mind.

"Rest?" I asked confusingly, looking at Ghamen for an explanation.

"Mummies, he thinks we are mummies, and that he woke us up," explained Ghamen.

"How dare you wake us!" stated Mayza in a deep voice, with her arms outstretched.

"Mayza! Stop fooling around," Ghamen said, pushing her arms back down to her sides.

"Okay, okay, I'm just playing," said Mayza in a pout.

"Please, just let me go!" cried the man.

"Calm down. We're not mummies," I said, desperately trying to reassure the poor man.

"Yes you are, and I've woken you. Please, take my broom. It's a good broom, just let me go," the man pleaded, offering up his broom.

"I don't want your broom. I want directions to the supply shop," I said, trying not to scare him.

"Directions?" asked the man, still holding out his broom.

"Yes. I need directions to the nearest supply shop," I said, glancing at Ghamen who was trying hard not to laugh.

"There is a shop not too far from here. You go that way," he said, pointing to his right.

The three of us looked at each other and shook our heads in agreement. I thanked the man who still insisted that we take his broom and we left. We headed out the door and back into the blazing sun, where a slight breeze made it easy for us to brush off the dust. We crept down the deserted street, looking into each hut we passed. Ghamen decided that it was best if we ran quickly from hut to hut, and then crept slowly around the front to look in. We stayed in single file and were careful not to make any noise because if we were spotted by the thieves, there wouldn't be much of a chance to recover the bag which had both the scrolls and the key. Our only hope was to find them before they found us and then to sneak the bag away from them without being noticed. That way we could disappear without a trace.

We passed seven huts before we saw one that had people outside of it. We hid behind a wall nearby and watched what was going on. I could tell that it was definitely a supply shop, because of all the items that were lying in front of it. There were sleeping mats, hunting tools and barrels of food for animals. There was a lot of commotion and I wasn't sure how we were ever going to get the bag back. We looked at each other in silence, and I signalled for Ghamen and I to take a closer look while Mayza stayed put to keep an eye out for any danger.

The two of us crawled along the dirt until we came to the side of the building. Ghamen pointed his finger up to a window ledge that he wanted me to peek through, to see if the thieves were actually there. I nodded my head, took a deep breath and slowly got to my knees, inching my head up until my eyes could see over the ledge. Inside the busy room, supplies were scattered all over the floor while others hung on the walls. There were also tables and chairs and I found that not only was this a supply store, but it was also a restaurant and sure enough in the corner of the room, the four thieves were enjoying their lunch and my knapsack lay just off to the side. I sank back down and took a deep breath. Getting the bag back was not going to be easy.

"Did you see them?" whispered Ghamen.

"Yes. They're eating lunch and they have the bag," I whispered back.

"What should we do?" Ghamen asked.

"I have an idea but it's a long shot," I said, staring at the sand, trying to envision my plan.

"What is it?" asked Ghamen.

"We'll have to go over it a couple of times. Let's get back to Mayza and then I'll tell you."

The two of us crawled back to where Mayza was hiding. We discussed the plan in detail and after a few preparations we were ready to roll. Like I said before, it was a long shot but it just might work.

18

Twinkle Toes

The three of us rehearsed the plan and when we were finally ready, Ghamen gave me a slap on the back and wished me good luck while covering his mouth to keep from laughing. Mayza gave me a wink and told me that I looked like a beautiful princess. I rolled my eyes and left for the supply shop. I had never done anything like this before, but I didn't feel as silly as I thought I would.

Everyone who'd been outside the shop was now inside, either settling up their bills or shovelling food and drink down their throats. This made it easy for me to go unnoticed so that I could position myself properly and put the plan into action. I moved to the entrance of the shop, took a deep breath and flung myself through the doorway. Everybody in the whole place turned around at the same time to look at who had just blown in. They all stared, eyes wide open and jaws on the floor. They were looking at Tommy T. Timson–the dancing girl.

I wore a long white dress with colourful beads laced throughout. Jewellery dangled from my neck, arms and ankles and Mayza had put lipstick, eye makeup and blush on my face. Ghamen had made me a long black wig with ribbons hanging to my waist and I held a tambourine-like instrument in one hand and a flower in the other. You may be wondering where we got all this stuff. Don't worry. Mayza took care of it and she told me that it was all paid for. So here I was, about to put on the show of my life in front of a group of the most disgusting looking men I had ever seen. I made my way through the silent crowd to the middle of the shop, slowly raised my tambourine and as it began to rattle, I started to dance.

I tapped my bracelets together, swaying my hips to the beat of the tambourine. I made my way through the tables, brushing by the men who were now enjoying the show. "Hey sweet cheeks!" one man yelled out, reaching for my waist as I passed by his table. I swiftly moved away from his sweaty palms and gave him a quick push back into his seat. The room cheered so I decided to play along and reached over his shoulder, grabbed a piece of bread from his table, took a small bite and tossed the rest in his lap. His neighbours roared with laughter while I backed away and continued to dance.

I did a quick twirl and raised my foot onto another man's chair. I grabbed a drink from his table and the hat from his head. I spun the hat on my finger and swallowed the drink, slamming the cup down and throwing the hat back on his head, while pretending to lean in for a kiss. The man closed his eyes and puckered his lips, awaiting a passionate smooch. I quickly retreated from the table and he opened his eyes to the teasing and taunting of his companions. "Kissy, kissy, kissy," one of them chanted. The table laughed heartily as the man lowered his head in shame.

I glanced over at the window and caught sight of Ghamen, who was waiting anxiously with a fishing pole that I had made with a stick and some stuff I had found in my pencil case. I winked at him to let him know that it was a good time to try and fish the bag out from the shop, but he shrugged his shoulders in frustration. Continuing to dance, I searched the shop for the bag and found it under the table where the thieves were eating. I realized that Ghamen wasn't going to be able to snag it on the hook unless I moved it into the open.

Tapping my bracelets and playing my instrument, I twisted and turned, dancing around the thieves' table. I managed to slide the bag out from under the table with my foot and kicked it towards Ghamen. The bag was now close enough for him to hook it, but now I really had to keep everyone's attention off the floor and away from the window. Ghamen was now ready to start fishing, so I made my way to the opposite end of the room and, THUMP, THUMP! I hiked up my dress, hopped onto a small table, kicked my feet and twirled around. The crowd stood in excitement, swinging their arms and shouting at the top of their lungs. If my sister ever found out about this, I would never be able to live it down.

Ghamen wound up and cast the line through the window. The hook flew through the air unnoticed by the patrons, but landed just short of the bag. I realized that this was going to be harder than we had imagined as I watched Ghamen carefully reel in the line for his second attempt. Strike two, I thought to myself as the hook fell short once again. I started to worry because my legs were getting tired and I didn't know how long I could keep this up before we would be discovered. I watched out of the corner of my eye as Ghamen made his third attempt. He leaned back, paused for a moment and then with all his strength he let the hook fly through the room. Sure enough, it landed right on the bag. We were almost in the clear, so I danced like no boy who had travelled back in time to Egypt and dressed like a girl had ever danced before. Ghamen carefully jerked the line until the hook had secured itself onto one of the straps and gently reeled it in while I kept the crowd busy with my delicate toes. Slowly but surely Ghamen was doing it, the plan was working, we were going to get the bag back!

"STOP EVERYTHING!" one of the thieves shouted, stomping his foot down on the bag. The crowd fell silent and the three other thieves walked over to see what the problem was. Ghamen had quickly disappeared but had left the pole hanging from the ledge. The thief, who had uncovered our plot, bent down and picked up the bag. He yanked it violently and the fishing pole flew towards him, landing at his feet.

"It has to be those kids! I thought you took care of them!" said the leader, picking up the pole and examining it. The three disgraced thieves stood in silence with their eyes to the floor. "Must I do everything myself?" he continued, grabbing the bag and making his way to the window. I was worried that he would spot Ghamen and Mayza so I started up with my tambourine again, but this time no one seemed to appreciate my musical genius. The leader turned around and shouted at his men to throw me out of the shop. Mayza must have done a really good job with my make up because they still hadn't suspected me.

Two of the thieves approached me but I knew that I couldn't leave the shop without my bag. I started to leap from table to table, avoiding the thieves as they tripped and stumbled around the chairs. The leader dropped his head in frustration and ridiculed them. "You useless fools! I should have left you all in the desert!" he shouted, lunging at me, causing me to lose my balance and fall to the floor. He grabbed my wig and yanked hard, hoping to pull me up, but the wig came off in his hand and he fell on his backside onto the floor. The three thieves snickered under their breath at the sight of their leader sitting on the floor, holding my long black wig. Dumbfounded, he slowly raised his eyes to meet mine and recognizing me, smiled a devilish grin and yelled at the top of his lungs, "GET HIM!"

The three thieves scattered, desperately trying to grab hold of me. I crawled through the tables and around the chairs. The remaining patrons in the shop, who had been sitting quietly throughout the last few moments, were now laughing as I crawled under their legs and through their feet trying to keep away from the thieves. Everywhere I turned, long yellow toe nails attached to long stinking toes attached to really hairy feet were in my face! UGH! I tried to hold my breath, but after all the dancing and now the crawling, I just couldn't do it. I saw my bag sitting on a table near the window and I decided to go for it.

The leader was now at the bar opposite the window. I wasn't sure where the others were so I got up, but one of them noticed and started to run at me. I dashed across the room, jumped onto a table, grabbed the bag and headed for the window.

"GET HIM you fools!" yelled the leader, as I hopped up onto the window ledge and leaped out of the shop.

"Over here, Tommy!" Mayza yelled, motioning towards a horse-drawn wagon that was just leaving the store. We chased after it and managed to jump into the back as it sped away.

NEIGGHH!

The commotion startled the horses, and they began to gallop furiously. The driver was thrown back into his seat. "What's going on?" the man yelled, grabbing the reins to control his scared animals.

Mayza yelled, "They're after us!" The driver turned and noticed the thieves mounting their horses, the leader viciously pointing his dagger at the wagon.

"Grab hold of something, kids, and hang on!" the driver cried out. "HIYA!"

19

WOOWEE!

We sat low in the cart, bracing ourselves so we wouldn't fall out of the back. Our plan didn't go exactly as we hoped, but we did come out with the bag and now all we had to do was get away from the thieves.

"Do you have the scrolls?" Ghamen yelled, over the sounds of the charging horses.

"They're right here!" I shouted back, showing him the bag that was hanging off my shoulder, while shedding my costume.

"Are you all right?" asked Mayza, while looking out the back of the cart.

"I'm fine. My wig came off and then everything went crazy," I explained.

We continued to cling to the sides of the cart. It was old but it was sturdy and it was moving quickly. The back was filled with papyrus stems and some long scraps of wood. The driver was an older man with long, messy grey hair that blew uncontrollably in the wind. I was surprised that he could even see where he was going with that mess on his head. His four horses pulled us along, speeding down the street, their hooves humming like the engine of a train.

"Hey kids, where are we going?" yelled the old man excitedly.

"We need to get to the palace just outside the city limits," explained Ghamen.

I looked at Ghamen in amazement. I couldn't believe how willing the driver was to help us. He hadn't even asked us why we were being chased by four thieves.

"So why are you being chased by four thieves?" he asked, flashing us a smile.

"How do you know they're thieves?" asked Mayza.

"When you spend enough time in these rough parts of town, you begin to know who's who. Besides, I saw them slipping fruit into their pockets, WOOWEE!" he chuckled, glancing back, flashing us another smile. I could tell that this guy was a little off his rocker, but we needed his help so I was willing to tolerate his insanity.

The thieves were fast approaching and I knew they would soon catch us. The wind was swirling around our heads and I looked for anything that I could throw at them, but there was nothing other than the papyrus stems and the long thin sticks which wouldn't be of any help.

"They're going to catch up to us!" I yelled to Ghamen and Mayza.

"I know," replied Ghamen.

"How far is the palace?" I asked.

"It's not too far from here," Ghamen replied, looking very worried. It was clear that the thieves were going to catch up to us before we would arrive at the palace and I could tell that none of us knew what we were going to do once they did.

We had only been riding for maybe two minutes, but the tension had built to an unbearable level. We were quiet, waiting for the inevitable moment when the thieves would hijack the cart and finish us off.

"HIYA!" screamed the old man, as he snapped the reins and ate a piece of fruit that he pulled out from under his seat. "Fruit anyone?" he asked, turning completely around to face us while abandoning the reins. The three of us looked at each other in shock. Was this guy for real? Had we accidentally jumped onto the loony train to Nuts Ville? "Nobody wants fruit," he continued. "What about you, little girl?" he asked, holding out the piece of fruit.

"What about the horses?" cried Mayza.

"The horses? I forgot!" he said, returning to the reins. "I'm getting old," he continued. "Starting to lose it up here, if you know what I mean," he said, pointing to his head. "WOOWEE!"

"Here they come," said Ghamen, getting to his knees, ready for their attack. Three of them surrounded the cart while the leader stayed back, shouting orders as he had always done so well.

"Grab the sticks and hit them if they get too close," I ordered, grabbing one myself. The three of us were now on our knees with sticks in hand, trying hard not to fall over. We were moving very fast and the cart shook from side to side which made it difficult to keep balanced. The three thieves moved in on us, and we got ready to defend the cart.

The first thief came up on the left side of the cart. He pulled close along the side and swiped his arm at us. "WOOWEE!" screamed the old man, steering his horses, causing the cart to sway back and forth. The three of us fell down and rolled around trying to get back to our knees. I grabbed the side of the cart and pulled myself up to peek over, only to see the thief returning for another attack. This time he came alongside us and stood on his saddle, crouching on the back of his horse. When he was close enough, he threw himself at the cart and landed with a thud that sent us flying back into the papyrus stems.

We looked up to find him climbing into the cart, so Ghamen and Mayza started whacking at his arm while I pushed his head back. Our driver turned to see what was going on and noticing that we had an unwanted passenger, swayed the cart back and forth. "WOOWEE!" he yelled in excitement, watching the thief dangle from the side of the wagon. "Watch out, kids!" the old man yelled, winding up and launching a piece of fruit that struck the thief in the head, causing him to lose his grip on the cart. The thief fell to the dirt, and rolled out of sight.

The three of us took deep breaths and prepared for the next attack. The second thief rode alongside the front of the cart where the old man was driving. From where we were kneeling, there was nothing we could do but watch. "WOOWEE!" screamed the driver repeatedly, teasing and taunting the thief. The old man was crazier than I thought and he was treating the whole thing like a game. He made faces at the thief and waved his arms around like a baboon. The thief got upset and his swipes became more vicious. He crouched onto his horse like the first had done and prepared to jump onto the cart. I tensed, waiting for him to mount the cart, but instead, the old man threw himself onto the thief's horse! The two struggled as the horse raced through the streets.

The three of us looked at each other in disbelief and then noticing that no one was driving the cart, screamed at the top of our lungs, "HOLY COW!"

"We're going to crash!" yelled Mayza.

"We're all going to die!" I added.

"That guy's the craziest person I've ever seen!" declared Ghamen, as loudly as he could.

We held on tight while the cart raced out of control through the city. I caught a glimpse of the old man who was still struggling with the thief, but right now that was the least of our worries.

"Ghamen," I shouted, "you have to climb up and take control!"

"Why me? Why can't you do it?" he shouted back.

"Because I don't know how to drive!" I answered.

"Look! Here he comes," Mayza interrupted. We all looked out the side and sure enough, the old man had managed to throw the thief off his horse and was returning to the cart. He pulled up alongside us and jumped back onto the cart. He moved to the front, grabbed hold of the reins and reached under his seat for another piece of fruit.

"Fruit anyone?" he asked calmly, as if we were all relaxing in the sun.

"NO!" we screamed back.

The cart stabilized and we regained our balance and looked out to see the remaining two thieves still close behind. "There are still two left," Mayza cried.

"I don't know what to do," I said, looking around the cart. "There's nothing to throw."

"We can throw Mayza," Ghamen said, smiling at his sister.

"You're the funniest person I ever met," replied Mayza, rolling her eyes, continuing to look for a weapon.

"Come on guys, we have to think," I said to them, looking out at the thieves who were only seconds away from attacking us.

"Anyone ever been in a sandstorm?" shouted the old man, from the front of the cart. The three of us looked at each other in anticipation of the nonsense we were expecting to hear from him. "Well, horses hate sandstorms. I say you take those sticks and drag them through the sand. Then you'll have one big storm on your hands."

We looked at each other, thinking about what the old man had said. Then we looked back and saw that the thieves were right behind us, so we scrambled to grab the long sticks and then carefully crawled to the edge of the cart. We lay flat on our stomachs and reached down with our sticks until they were touching the sand. The old man was right! As soon as the sticks touched the ground the sand began to fly. The three of us dragged our sticks from side to side, causing a sandstorm that was becoming thicker by the second. The two thieves had fallen behind and were slowly disappearing in the cloud.

"We're almost at the palace," yelled the old man. "I'm just going to slow down, so you kids get ready to jump!"

"Slow down?" yelled Ghamen.

"Jump?" yelled Mayza.

I got to my knees and peered over the front of the cart. I could see the large palace and all the activity that surrounded it. There were small buildings scattered throughout the area, and not far off were two giant pyramids. This was the closest I had ever been to a pyramid and the sight of them made me completely forget that I was about to jump from a moving cart.

"Alright kids. Get ready to jump. WOOWEE!" said the old man, who was laughing hysterically.

I looked back and could still see the thieves chasing us. They had lost ground during our man-made sandstorm. The old man pulled the cart over and to our relief came to a complete stop. "Good luck kids," the old man said, smiling at us. We thanked him quickly, jumped out the back and watched him speed off, hollering, "WOOWEE!"

"Where to?" I asked.

"Over there," Ghamen said, pointing across the street.

"Hurry! The thieves are back," Mayza cried. We looked and to our surprise all four of them were running towards us, the leader shouting at his men to catch us. The chase became a foot race as we dashed up the stairs to the entrance of the palace with the sounds of footsteps close behind. The thieves were much faster than we were and we knew it was only a matter of time before they'd catch us. I took a deep breath and followed my two desperate friends into the building.

20

The Verdict Is . . .

We ran through the entrance of the palace, frantically looking for any signs of where their mother might be. It was crowded and buzzing with activity which made managing the halls difficult. None of us could see very far ahead, so finding her wasn't going to be easy. We ran down the corridors taking the corners as sharply as we could, in an effort to lose the thieves, but they stayed close.

"Do you know where you're going?" I yelled out to Ghamen, as we flew around another corner.

"I've been here once before. I think it's at the end of this hall," he said, as we ran full tilt, weaving through the crowd. "There it is!" Ghamen exclaimed, as we approached two solid doors with large golden handles. I looked over my shoulder and could see one of the thieves approaching fast. We were out of time and if this wasn't the right room–we were finished.

BOOM! Ghamen burst through the doors with Mayza and me following close behind. Guards were standing on the other side of the doors and immediately stopped us from entering any further. The thieves followed right behind us with looks of terror on their faces as they saw more guards waiting with open arms. They tried to stop but they were running so fast that it was no use, and in seconds we had all been apprehended.

"Mother!" cried Ghamen and Mayza, trying madly to free themselves from the grip of the guards. Across the room, I could see their mom who got up from her chair, and lunged towards Ghamen and Mayza, tears streaming down her face.

"Mayza, Ghamen are you all right?" she cried, as two guards forced her back into her seat.

"What's the meaning of all this?" shouted the head official, furiously pounding the butt of his staff onto the floor. "How dare you interrupt," he continued. "Guards! Throw these people out of here!"

"Wait!" yelled Ghamen. "WE HAVE THE SCROLLS!" The head official looked at us sternly and turned to his **scribe** who was sitting beside him in a very upright position. The two talked quietly for a moment and then the head official looked back at us.

"Show me them!" he demanded. Ghamen took the bag from my shoulder and unzipped it with ease, reached in, grabbed the scrolls and handed them to him. A hush fell over the room as the head official unrolled the scrolls to examine them. After looking them over, he asked, "Where did you get these?"

"I retrieved them from those thieves," he said, pointing back around.

"Isn't she your mother?" the head official asked, motioning to the lady in the chair.

"Yes, sir," replied Ghamen.

"Why should I believe you? Maybe you were given these by your mother," he said, while scratching his chin.

"That's not true!" yelled Ghamen. "My mother didn't steal anything!" Ghamen's reaction to the head official's speculation caused a murmur through the crowd.

"Quiet!" he ordered. The scribe, who had been sitting quietly, suddenly leaned over and whispered to the head official. The room fell silent as everyone waited in anticipation for what was to come. The scribe returned to his upright position and the head official stood to address the crowd.

"Information has come to light as to the identity of the three men who are being held in front of me. They belong to a gang of bandits led by the notorious thief known as the Dark Beetle. I want them arrested! Guards! Take them away and find the leader!" he said, raising his hand and pointing to the door. "As for you," he continued, turning to speak to Ghamen and Mayza's mother. "I see no further reason for this trial. You have always been a loyal servant to the Pharaoh and I now declare you free."

The crowd cheered as a guard unlocked the chains that bound the woman. Their mother descended from the platform where she had been sitting and Ghamen and Mayza both ran to meet her. The three of them hugged and kissed in a joyful reunion that almost made me cry, but I didn't cry. I almost cried, but I didn't.

"Oh dearest children, I thought I would never see you again," she said, hugging them with all her strength.

"I love you, mother," they said, holding her tightly, tears streaming down their faces.

"I am so proud of you. You saved us. You brave children," she said, loosening her grip to look at them closely.

"Saved US?" replied Ghamen, looking at his mother questioningly.

"Yes. Your father and me," she said with a smile, turning her head towards a door that slowly opened, revealing their dad who had been detained separately. Mayza and Ghamen looked at him in astonishment as he appeared in the doorway and calmly approached them with a warm smile. He was tall and looked like a strong man. His eyes were a soft brown and he moved gently, unlike anyone I had seen since arriving in Egypt.

"Father!" they cried, running to greet him. "We thought you were dead," they continued, jumping into his arms.

"They just got a piece of me," he said, revealing a bandage on his chest. "Now come to me. I missed both of you so much," he continued, lifting them off the ground and twirling them, giving them both big kisses. Mayza and Ghamen were filled with tears of joy and that's when I started crying. Their father carried them to their mother and the four of them hugged each other tightly.

They were so happy, and it made me think of my family and how much I missed them. If I could only be reunited with them, I'd be the happiest kid in the world. I missed my family so much that I thought I would cry forever. That's when I remembered that I hadn't checked the time since I'd been locked in the sarcophagus. My heart stopped and sweat oozed from my pores. Had I missed the door? I felt my wrist burn under my watch. I needed somewhere private enough so that I could check it without being noticed. I started to panic and shot a look at Mayza who understood right away what I was trying to say.

"This is our friend, Tommy," said Mayza, escorting me by the hand to meet her parents.

"Hello, Tommy, it is a pleasure to meet you," said her mother, touching my shoulder.

"He helped us escape from the thieves and return the scrolls," Ghamen said, smiling at his mother.

"Thank you for your help. We will always remember your kindness," said their father, squeezing Ghamen who was still in his arms. I didn't know what to say, so I just smiled, when two guards quickly rushed into the room and notified the head official that the leader had escaped.

"How can they let him get away? He kidnapped us and had you thrown in jail!" Ghamen said in anger.

"Ghamen," replied his father, "he may have escaped for now, but the good that has come from each of your actions can never be overshadowed by the evil of that man. You all showed courage and saved us. That is what is important. One day his deeds will catch up with him and he will be punished, but until that day comes, we have to learn to put him aside and enjoy our new lives together." Ghamen smiled at his father's words and slowly his anger left him. Ghamen's father hugged him and continued, "The three of you can also be proud of the fact that you have saved the tomb of **Tutankhamen** from being looted. Now that the scrolls have been returned, his tomb will be safe forever."

Tutankhamen! Wow! I know who that is. Last summer I saw an exhibit at the museum all about him and his tomb. I stood in wonderment, realizing that I had been carrying the scrolls that held the secrets to the tomb of King Tut! I knew the tomb wouldn't be safe forever, but at least I helped preserve it for a few thousand years.

The five of us made our way out of the palace and onto the steps. I still hadn't checked the time and was becoming more anxious with each passing moment. When we arrived on the steps of the palace, their parents asked me if I would come to their house for the evening. Ghamen answered quickly, saying my own mother expected me and that I had to leave. I thanked them for their offer and then we said our good-byes. Mayza and Ghamen told them that they were going to walk me down the stairs and see me off. Their parents waved me a final good-bye and the three of us walked quickly to the street.

When we reached the bottom of the stairs, I asked Mayza and Ghamen to huddle around me so that I could check the time. They blocked me so nobody could see and then I took a breath, lowered my eyes and looked at my watch. It was 2:45 pm! I only had thirty minutes to get to the door and I still didn't know where to find it.

"I'm late! I have to find the pyramid!" I said, as my heart raced.

"Relax, Tommy. It is right over there," Ghamen said, pointing off into the near distance. I looked over and saw the pyramid not too far off. A wave of relief washed over me knowing that it wouldn't take long to get there.

"Okay, I can still make it," I said, trying to slow my heartbeat.

"I guess it's time for you to go," said Ghamen. "Thank you for all you have done for our family," he continued. "We will never forget you."

"If it weren't for the two of you, I wouldn't have had a chance to make it this far," I responded. "You guys have been really good friends."

"Be careful, Tommy," Mayza said, giving me a hug.

"Thanks, Mayza. Thanks, Ghamen," I said, hugging them good-bye. The three of us stood in silence, knowing that this would be the last time we would ever see each other. Usually when people say good-bye, it's not for good and that's what made this different. The three of us had been through so much and although I'd only known them for less than a day, it seemed longer to all of us. We looked at each other not knowing how to express the way we felt, but I think the silence we shared spoke for us all. We each said a last good-bye and then I turned around to leave.

"Tommy!" I turned back around to see Mayza, who ran to me and gently kissed me on the lips. "Good luck," she said, quickly retreating back to her brother. WOW! I was stunned and didn't know how to react. That was the best thing that had happened to me all day! I looked up and watched the two of them make their way back to their parents as Ghamen teased Mayza for kissing me. I snapped out of my daze, turned around and hurried off towards the pyramid.

21

Enter At Your Own Risk

It didn't take long to arrive at the pyramid and although I had been through so much in the last day, I had to remind myself that it wasn't over and that my true test of courage was about to begin.

I stopped at the foot of the pyramid and looked up as the sun glistened off the walls that climbed to the sky above. Thousands of stone blocks sat layer upon layer, precisely carved to fit into its massive frame.

"This better be it," I said aloud, quickly making my way towards the small opening that had been clumsily boarded up. Over the entrance, as I'd seen in my textbook, were the four carved symbols shining in the sun. I took off my knapsack and retrieved the key and my jacket. I put my jacket on and compared the markings on the key with those above the entrance. They matched!

I placed the key back in my bag and kicked in the boards. I checked my watch; it was 2:55 pm which meant that I had to get moving. Inside it was dark and just before sliding through the boards, I checked to make sure that I was alone and took one last look for Percival, but he was nowhere in sight. I took a deep breath and made my way in.

It was very dark and it took a while for my eyes to adjust. A small bit of light from the entrance lit the inside just enough so that I could see. I looked ahead and saw three tunnels that went off in different directions. I figured that only one would lead to the tomb but which one, I didn't know. I thought for a moment and then chose the logical approach to decision making. ". . . eany, meany, miney, MOE." I chose the tunnel to my left and started on my way, but after only a few short steps, I was in total darkness and I wasn't able to see a thing. I stopped for a moment and then pushed the light button on my watch. "Alright," I sighed, as my light brightened the tunnel just enough so that I could see in front of me.

I continued down the dark passageway, every step echoing through the emptiness of the pyramid, when out of the corner of my eye I saw the shadow of a figure standing against the wall. I froze and watched as it streaked into the darkness, vanishing out of sight. I nervously called out to it, but there was nothing there. It was gone! I walked to where it had been and in its place, lay a stone in the shape of an egg. I picked it up and turned it over. WOW! The four symbols were carved on the side! I smiled, knowing that I was on the right track and put it in my pocket.

I walked down several tunnels that seemed to go on forever and I started to get scared and ran frantically, using my hand as a guide along the cold walls of the pyramid. In the darkness, I turned right and then left and then tripped over something and fell hard on a pile of sharp sticks and rocks. Confused and scared, I sat up and turned on my light. To my horror, what I had thought were sticks and stones were actually the skeletons of those who tried to reach the tomb before me. I screamed and jumped up as fast as I could, wiping the dust from my body. I ran back the way I'd come as quickly as I could to get away from the bones, but now I had completely lost my way and was too scared to go on.

I stopped to catch my breath. Then I saw a light shining in the distance. It flickered for a few seconds and then disappeared. I stared deep into the darkness trying to find it, when all of a sudden I felt a tap on my right shoulder that made me jump ten feet! I turned around but nobody was there. My heart was racing and I tried to catch my breath. Then, in the distance, I saw the flickering light again, but this time it was coming from the opposite direction. "Hello!" I yelled to whatever it was, but all I heard in return was the echo of my own voice. I watched as the light bobbed up and down and then it started to come towards me. I tried to take a step back but my feet wouldn't move. They were stuck to the ground! "HELP!" I screamed, trying to free them.

Suddenly, a loud rumbling noise shook the inside of the tunnel and two stone walls rose from the ground, boxing me in. I crouched down in fear and covered my head for protection as dust and stone fell from the ceiling. The rumbling became louder and louder and then suddenly there was silence. I raised my head and turned my light on. I was completely trapped on all sides. My feet were free, so I pushed against one of the walls but it wouldn't budge.

I tried another but it was no use. "HELP!" I screamed at the top of my lungs, desperately feeling around the bumps and grooves of the walls in search of an opening.

I checked my watch. It was 3:05 pm! I turned my light off and in total darkness, sank down to the base of the wall, feeling completely lost, knowing that the end had come and soon I'd be nothing more than the latest addition of bones to the pyramid's skeletal exhibit. I sat in silence awaiting my doom when I heard a sound. I raised my head again and peered into the darkness.

DRIP!

I turned my light on and made my way towards the noise. DRIP! I looked down and saw a puddle forming from droplets that were falling from above my head.

DRIP! DRIP!

I got down on a knee and dipped two fingers into the puddle, raised them to my nose and smelled. It was water, but where was it coming from? I stared deeply into the puddle when an image slowly appeared. It was faint, but it looked like a baby being held in the arms of a mother. I stared in amazement as the image changed to a boy running through a field and then to a grown man and then finally to an image of an elderly man sitting in a chair. I kept looking at the puddle but the image slowly faded out, leaving only the water on the ground.

I sat back and tried to figure out what the images were trying to tell me. I stood up and looked around the room for anything that could help me find the hidden tomb. I checked my watch which said 3:07 pm! Time was running out and I was getting really scared. "Where is the tomb?" I asked the puddle, and to my relief a written message appeared in the water.

You have already found it.

I shrugged my shoulders and shook my head in frustration. "I haven't found anything! I'm trapped in a pyramid!" Another message appeared.

Don't let your eyes deceive you.
Your answer lies within these walls.

I stood in the stone box thinking about the messages when suddenly the rumbling returned and the walls began to shake. Frightened, I crouched down again and covered my head. This time I really thought I was a goner. I held on tight, but soon the rumbling stopped and I opened my eyes slowly, finding myself in the most magnificent room I had ever seen–the great burial chamber of the ancient leader.

22

Race Against Time

The small stone box had transformed into a brilliant tomb, warmly lit with torches that hung on the walls, illuminating beautiful artwork that graced the room. Scattered on the ground were priceless golden statues, jewels and beautiful boxes. In the middle of the tomb lay the sarcophagus of the ancient leader. It stood imposingly in front of me, displaying its intricate carvings with pride. I walked up to the coffin and ran my hand across its surface, thinking about all who had tried but failed to reach it. I looked down and at its side against the wall I saw a statue of a cat much like the one that had found my watch. I knelt down and touched its head and then noticed a boat and a raft that looked the same as the ones we had travelled on. They were made of stone and I picked up the raft and stood up. I looked closely and inside sat three smiling kids. I put down the raft and continued to explore the tomb.

I looked closely at the artwork and designs on the walls and stopped when I saw a sketch of a clock. It was the same clock that I had in my bedroom and now I was looking at it on the wall inside the chamber and it read 3:10 pm. I looked at my own watch and it also said 3:10 pm! I only had five minutes!

I turned from the wall and began to quickly scour the tomb, looking for the door. I searched everywhere but couldn't find any trace of it. Out of breath, I stopped and stared at the sarcophagus. I suspected that it may have been hiding the door but I was still afraid to open it. The last thing I needed right now was to come face to face with a rotting corpse, but I knew that if I wanted to get home I had to exhaust all my options. I approached it slowly, aware of the time ticking down and grabbed hold of the lid. With my eyes shut I heaved with everything I had, but it wouldn't move. I tried again and again but I couldn't open the lid!

I gave up and looked around one more time for anything that looked like a door. That's when I caught sight of an old scale that had been sitting beside the sarcophagus. I took a closer look and on one end of it rested an oval stone just like the one I had picked up earlier. I quickly searched my pockets for the stone and placed it on the other end of the scale and stood back.

Slowly the two stones aligned and as the scale balanced a flash of light erupted so blinding that I was forced to cover my eyes. When the light had dimmed I lowered my hand and watched as the scale disappeared right before me and in its place was a piece of folded papyrus. I picked it up, opened it, and began to read.

The Greatest Riddle of All Time

I am a gift like no other;
You cannot measure my worth.
I've been with you since the beginning;
I'll be with you until the end.
I make you what you are,
But you make me what I am.
Find me and decide our fate.

I scratched my head and checked my watch. It was 3:12 pm and I had to figure this out fast or I would be stuck in this tomb forever! I went over the riddle in my head, rearranging the words in different ways, but water was dripping into the puddle again and it was driving me crazy. I tried to block it out, but the drips, like the seconds on my watch, seemed to quicken and pound in my head. Time was ticking and the nervousness in my stomach grew. I blocked my ears and kept my eyes on the riddle but I couldn't take it anymore and finally I turned to the puddle and yelled, "STOP!"

Sure enough the drops stopped falling and another message appeared in the water. I walked over, bent down and read.

Clear your mind. Your answer lies within.

I watched closely as the images that I had seen earlier returned. They appeared in sequence starting with the baby and ending with the old man. The images repeated themselves over and over again. Eventually, I realized that I was looking at myself going through all the stages of life. I watched myself change from a newborn to a child and then to a grown man and finally to the old man in the chair. The sight of me as an old man made me smile, because for an old man, I was still unusually handsome. The cycle of images sped up to a blur and then disappeared.

I stood in amazement. Having your life flash before your eyes was a lot to take in, especially seeing things that were yet to happen. That's when it hit me!

"That's it! I've got it!" I cheered. "LIFE! Life is the answer! Life is a gift like no other! Its worth can never be measured and life is with me from beginning to end! Life is what we make it!"

I was so excited about the riddle that I had completely forgotten about the time. I looked down at my watch. It was *a quarter past three*! "THE DOOR!" I screamed, and began to search the room furiously. I threw the artifacts aside and looked under anything I could find. I stepped up on a stool and checked behind the sarcophagus but it wasn't there. I took a step back from the coffin and noticed a bright golden lock that hadn't been there before. I retrieved my key, placed it in the lock, and turned. I held my breath, hoping I had solved the riddle correctly and pulled at the lid of the sarcophagus. The heavy lid creaked open and inside rested the frayed mummy wrappings of the great tribal leader. I jumped back in fear and grabbed the lid to slam it shut when I noticed another papyrus letter sitting on the mummy's chest. I grabbed the paper and started to read.

Your life is the most amazing gift you will ever receive. The most beautiful treasure ever known, is realizing how special life is, and living each day to the fullest.

This was the answer! I was right! I had solved the riddle, and just then, the body of the great leader disintegrated and the inside of the sarcophagus glowed brightly. I HAD found the magical door! I took one last look around the ancient tomb and before jumping inside, I bid farewell to a journey I would never forget and to two friends I would always remember. I folded the letter and placed it inside my pocket. I then climbed inside the sarcophagus and closed the lid behind me.

23

Where In The World Am I Now?

"Here we go AGAIIINNNN!" A whirlwind of infinite colours swept me up into a vacuum of howling winds. "AAAHHH!" My arms and legs flailed all around as I spun out of control towards the earth below. "EARTH BELOW?" Oh no! I was free-falling through the clouds, the wind stretching my face as I sped towards the ground. This didn't happen last time! I fell faster and faster and as I dropped, I noticed something racing up towards me. I heard a screaming voice coming at me, as someone zipped past me in the opposite direction, scaring me half to death. "WHAT'S GOING OOONNN?" Then without warning it all stopped.

I appeared in the middle of a crowd that was standing at the base of a giant archway that served as the entrance to a beautiful palace. The palace was surrounded by tall red walls with soldiers wearing shiny helmets and holding long spears standing high on top. Bright yellow flags with dragons flapped violently in the wind, and the sound of clashing cymbals rang through the air. Through the archway, I could see a platform that had been decorated with more of the yellow dragon flags. The crowd was inching its way forward, but was being held back by other soldiers that pushed against the group with their long spears. They were preventing the crowd from passing through the giant archway, whose doors were also red and decorated with countless golden knobs. I was caught in the flow and forced ahead when I lost my footing and fell to the ground. I tried to get up but the crowd was too thick. I struggled beneath the wave of people, trying madly to avoid the blows from their feet, when suddenly I was taken by the hand and hauled to my feet.

"PERCIVAL! Where were you?" I yelled in surprise.

"Tommy, there's NO time to explain! Something's gone wrong!"

"But . . ."

"No Tommy! Just follow me!" he said, grabbing my arm and weaving me through the mob of people. As he led me out of the crowd, the clashing of the cymbals grew louder. I looked towards the palace and could see an elaborately dressed old man, being escorted onto the platform by a group of soldiers. The crowd cheered as he raised his arms. Where in the world was I now?

GLOSSARY OF ANCIENT EGYPTIAN WORDS

Anubis: (noun) an Egyptian god of the dead, represented as part jackal or dog, part human.

embalming: (verb) to preserve (a corpse) from decay by the application of ointments, resins, etc. or by injections.

Great Pyramid: (noun) the huge pyramid of King Khufu at Giza is one of the Seven Wonders of the Ancient World.

hieroglyphics: (noun) method of writing in which a symbol, usually pictorial, represents a word, syllable or sound.

Memphis: (noun) an ancient town of N. Egypt. It was the capital of Egypt (3100-2100 BC).

mummification: (noun) to embalm and dry (a body) so as to preserve it. To wrap up, etc. like a mummy.

Nile River: (noun) a river of Africa, the world's longest, flowing from the equator to the Mediterranean. Its delta, beginning at Cairo, is 120 miles wide.

papyrus: (noun) an aquatic plant indigenous to the Nile Valley. The pith, shredded and pressed into sheets, was used to write on.

Pharaoh: (noun) the title of Ancient Egyptian kings (Egyptian for "great house"). Beginning in the 18th Dynasty, it was applied to the king himself.

pyramid(s): (noun) large square-based stone monuments constructed by the Ancient Egyptians as royal burial places, especially during the Old Kingdom (2614-2181 BC).

King Rameses II: (noun) king of Egypt (1290-1223 BC), of the 19th Dynasty.

Sais: (noun) an ancient city of Egypt on the Nile delta. It was the center of a brilliant civilization.

sarcophagus: (noun) a stone coffin usually ornamented.

scribe: (noun) a person skilled in handwriting, especially one who copied out manuscripts before the invention of printing. One of the most important officials in Ancient Egypt.

Thebes: (noun) an ancient city of Upper Egypt on the Nile. It was the capital of the Middle Kingdom.

tomb(s): (noun) a burial chamber–stone construction within or under which a person lies buried.

Tutankhamen: (noun) Egyptian king (1352-1343 BC) of the 18th Dynasty. At about the age of 9, he became the youngest Pharaoh ever, ruling until his death at about the age of 18. His tomb, discovered in 1922 was almost intact near Thebes.

Valley of the Kings: (noun) gorge on the western bank of the Nile River, Southern Egypt. It was the burial site of Pharaohs of the New Kingdom (1570-1070 BC).

SPECIAL THANKS

We would like to thank all those who helped in the process of putting this book together: Gerry Hooper, Theresa Kelly, Frieda Fraser, Carolyn Carson, Joe LeClair, Emily Brascoupe, Raymond Coderre, Victor Tsao, Anthony Whalen and Roberta Shaw (Assistant Curator–Egyptian Section–Royal Ontario Museum).

COVER ILLUSTRATION – Dominic Bercier was born in Ottawa and raised in Treadwell/North Plantagenet before returning to the capital, eventually studying art in high school. He pursued his studies in painting and illustration at Ontario College of Art and Design in Toronto, where he now lives with his wife, Isabelle and cat, Magie. His illustration and design company, PopTerra, makes images for books, comics, storyboards and anything else that would not be without a new story visual.

COVER DESIGN – Jeremy Axon was born and raised in Burlington and currently studies linguistics at York University. He has designed for clients in the software, retail, furniture, beverage, and movie industries-and now for the publishing industry as well with his work as a designer for PopTerra. He currently lives in Toronto with his two cats, Okami and Emma.

PopTerra – *new story visuals*
(416) 656-9430   d@popterra.com